Assassin

The Stopper Files, Volume 4

Eugene Lloyd MacRae

Published by Eugene Lloyd MacRae, 2018.

ASSASSIN

First edition. December 7, 2018.

Copyright © 2018 Eugene Lloyd MacRae.

ISBN: 978-1393980230

Written by Eugene Lloyd MacRae.

Chapter 1

LES SALONS HOCHE, PARIS, France

IT WAS A PARTY THAT WOULD END DRAMATICALLY.
Director Aubrey Laurent led the way, weaving in and out of the crowd and away from the dance floor to the bar. His girlfriend, Evelyn O'Toole, was right behind him. The laughter and conversation around them in the mauve and crystal ballroom was light and cheerful. Glasses clinked and the air was filled with the scent of deviled eggs with pickled shrimp, salmon caviar sushi and a dozen other hors d'oeuvres carried around by waiters dressed in a black tux or a young hostess dressed in a long sequined gown that matched with the decor. On the far side of the room, A Touch Of Paris ended its French chanson song and launched into one of its cabaret numbers

Evelyn looked back over her shoulder, "Oh, Aubrey, I want to dance to this one."

Laurent laughed as he glanced back, "Sorry, my brain says yes, my legs say please don't."

"You're a party poop."

"No, my legs are. Just give me a few minutes of rest."

The silver-haired woman smiled and pushed him playfully on the back, "And a gallon of alcohol for fuel."

"You know me so well," Laurent answered as he threaded his way to the twin lines of thirsty party-goers.

A dark-haired woman in a black chiffon dress, a loose v-neck sweater, and a black clutch bag fell in step just to the right of Evelyn.

Evelyn glanced at the woman, one eyebrow raising as she took in the dress and the sweater that hugged her body like an advertising banner.

The woman's eyes shifted left and she gave Evelyn a brief semi-smile before she took several long strides in her high heels.

Laurent came to a stop at the back of the left line of six couples and glanced to his right. He was surprised to see the woman standing there wasn't Evelyn.

Evelyn came to a stop behind Aubrey, scowling as she eyed the woman.

Glancing over his right shoulder at Evelyn, Laurent's eyebrows knit together, wondering why she was back there and not beside him. "Do you want your usual strawberry daiquiri?"

Taking a step to the left and then forward, Evelyn slipped her hand around his elbow, "Pardon?" She leaned forward and scowled again at the woman.

Shaking his head and giving her a smile, Laurent said, "I was asking if you wanted your usual–?" Laurent felt something and he looked down at his right hand. The back of it was covered with deviled eggs and pickled shrimp, "What the...?"

"Oh, I am so sorry, Monsieur." The dark-haired woman held a smashed hors-d'oeuvre in her left hand.

Laurent looked into her dark eyes, amused at the incident, "That's all right. It will come off. At least it avoided the suit." He held his hand up to look at the mess as his left reached for his pocket handkerchief, "Good thing I hand fold these."

The woman quickly flipped her clutch bag open and deposited the smashed hors d'oeuvre inside, "Oh, no, Monsieur. Let me. I have a moist towelette."

Laurent's eyebrows knit together in amusement when he saw the mess disappear into the expensive-looking sequined bag.

Evelyn leaned forward again, looking across at the woman Laurent was talking to. Her eyes flashed and narrowed.

Pulling something from the sequined bag, the woman said, "I will wipe it away."

Moving back, Evelyn nearly bumped into another couple joining the line, "I'm sorry. Excuse me." She slid to her right behind Laurent, wondering what was going on between him and the woman.

Slipping the sequined bag under her arm, the woman reached out and took Laurent's wrist while she used her gloved hand to place the moist towelette on his hand to wipe away the mess.

Evelyn's eyes shot open in alarm and she elbowed the woman away, grabbing Laurent's wrist herself, "Is that shrimp? He's allergic–" She cursed under her breath as she put her body against Laurent, put an arm around his waist and turned him, "C'mon, let's get that cleaned off before you start reacting."

Laurent laughed, "I'm fine, I'm fine. It's on the outside. I didn't swallow it."

"That's not the point." She cursed under her breath again, as she hustled him to the end of the bar and a stack of napkins.

Looking over his shoulder, Laurent looked to where the woman had been but he didn't see her.

Evelyn called to one of the bartenders, "Do you have some water? Water. I need water." She put a hand to her forehead, thinking. Then she said, "Une bouteille d'eau."

"Ah, oui." The bartender reached out with a bottle of water.

Grabbing the water, Evelyn unscrewed the top and held the bottle against a napkin. Setting the bottle down, she began to clean the mess off his hand, "How in the world did this happen?"

"I guess that woman beside me had it in her hand and it mashed against me."

Evelyn's eyes flashed as she wrapped the hors-d'oeuvre in the napkin and dropped the ball on the bar. Grabbing another napkin, she wet it and returned to wiping his hand.

"You aren't jealous, are you?"

"Did you bring your autoinjector?"

Laurent scoffed, "I'm fine. You worry too much."

Evelyn looked up at him as she continued wiping, "Which is your way of saying you didn't bring it. You know you're supposed to."

Looking off to where the woman had been again, Laurent smiled and said in a teasing voice, "She was beautiful, wasn't she?"

Wrinkling her nose, Evelyn continued wiping, "If you like all that heavy makeup kind of thing."

Laurent chuckled.

Evelyn looked up at Laurent without raising her head, "She had more lipstick, mascara, and blush than Estee Lauder and Christian Dior combined."

Smiling with affection, Laurent paced a finger under Evelyn's chin to raise her head slightly, "You don't have to worry. You're the one–" His hand dropped to his side. His eyes rolled back in his head. A moment later, Laurent crashed backward to the floor.

"Aubrey!"

Men and women rushed to help.

Evelyn dropped to one knee beside Laurent, putting a hand on his chest and one to his cheek, turning his head, "Aubrey? Aubrey? Can you hear me–?" Her jaw went slack. Her eyes rolled back in her head.

In slow motion, Evelyn O'Toole collapsed on top of Director Aubrey Laurent.

Chapter 2

OTTAWA, CANADA

THE AIR WAS CRISP AND CLEAR and the black water was rushing under the foot-thick ice when Merlin Arthur Dragon went into a panic. He reached out and his arm snaked around her waist, keeping her from dropping face down in a dangerous fall.

Jaimee Hartman giggled, grabbed onto the sleeve of his jacket and pulled herself upright again. She fell forward, wrapping her arms around his neck as her chest slapped against his, "Whoops." Her bright blue eyes sparkled as she looked up into his, "Thank you for saving me again, Mr. Dragon."

Merlin wrapped his arms around her willowy body, "Are you sure you want to keep doing this?"

"Yes." Pushing herself upright again, Jamie held onto his hand as she turned on her skates.

Merlin's arm stretched outward as he held her hand firmly. Jamie had asked him to help her with her skating and she had suggested the Rideau Canal, where the season had been extended a week into spring because the ice thickness had remained safe. At 7.8 kilometers long - nearly 5 miles and the surface equivalent of 90 Olympic-sized hockey rinks - it was billed as the world's longest and most romantic skating rink. It had five rest areas where you could find picnic tables, fire pits, and food vendors. You could rent skates at $18 for every 2 hours you wanted to be on the ice. Or you could rent a red sleigh. A few couples were skating hand-in-hand in the distance. But the most interesting fact for Merlin was the figure skating outfit Jamie wore. It was purple, with rhinestones, sequins and a short, frilly skirt, and she had chosen to wear transparent tights on her legs. He had to admit they made her long legs–

"Do you like my legs, Mr. Dragon?"

Merlin looked up to see a coy smile on her face. Her eyes looked at him with anticipation. Merlin cleared his throat, "Uh–"

His cell phone rang.

Jamie's smile turned to a frown, "Not again. Just when we were getting somewhere."

Merlin tugged on her hand and pulled her back to him, "Sorry. Hold on to me. I have to answer this."

Letting out a sigh, Jamie held onto his sleeve again, "Of course you do."

Pulling out his cell phone, Merlin looked at it. His special cell phone was connected to Interpol's I-24/7 secure global police network. It also contained a profile of his facial features and the advanced facial recognition software automatically unlocked the special features. That told him the call was coming in on a secure network and had to do with his role as Interpol's one and only Stopper, tasked with doing whatever was necessary to complete his assignments. He put the phone to his ear, "Hello?"

The female voice that came across sounded groggy and far away, "Mr. Dragon...?"

"Yes."

There was just a moment of silence.

"Who is this?"

The smacking sounds of someone with a dry mouth trying to get words out came across the phone.

Jamie let go of his sleeve and moved away from him. The crisp cold air was filled with the sounds of steel skate blades cutting across ice.

Closing his eyes against the sound, Merlin concentrated and listened, "Hello?"

"Yes...." The speech was slurred. "This is...Evelyn O'Toole. I met you...when...."

Merlin searched his mind. Then it came to him, "That day I was hired by–" He cut himself off, conscious of Jaimie overhearing him.

"Yes. That's right...Aubrey...Director Laurent...you were there to...."

"I remember." There was silence again. Then the sounds of steel blades cutting smoothly and sharply into the ice whirled right around him and Merlin closed his eyes again, concentrating, listening....

The voice came across again, thin and reedy, "I'm...I'm with CSIS...assigned to Interpol...." The words faded again.

Merlin wondered where this conversation was going. CSIS was the Canadian Security Intelligence Service - the country's spy agency - and he had never been told anything about Laurent's girlfriend. Mainly because it didn't matter. It was none of his business. He heard the smacking sounds again, and another sound - no, make that sounds, plural - the clicking and beeping of infusion pumps and heart monitors in an Intensive Care Unit. His heart jumped with fear, "Mz. O'Toole? Are you all right? Is–?"

"No. Contact Powless. Novichok."

"Pardon?" Merlin closed his eyes, listening, his mind massaging the words. Who was Powless? And the other word...Nova–?

A faint male voice sounded on the other side of the call, "Infirmière? Comment a-t-elle eu ce téléphone? Pouvez-vous l'obtenir? Cela pourrait interférer avec l'électronique."

Merlin felt panic. French? The accent didn't sound Québécois. And the words? They were faint and said fast - it sounded like thr man had said 'the phone would interfere with'...what? The electronics? Nothing made sense. He had no idea where she was or what was happening or what she wanted, "Hello? Mz. O'Toole? Hello?"

There was the sound of faint protest, the phone seemed to rustle, like two people were fighting over it, and then the groggy voice sounded again, "Russian nerve agent. Contact Pow—"

The line went dead.

Merlin looked at the phone, scratching his chin, thinking.

Jamie's voice cut through his thoughts, "I suppose you have to leave again?"

Looking up, Merlin opened his mouth to answer. The words never came out.

Nonchalantly, the inside edges of her skates cutting a clean line in a tight turn, Jamie Hartman turned into a backward glide, did a jump from a back inside edge of one skate, rotated in the air in the direction of the curve and landed smoothly on the back outside edge.

Merlin blinked. She had just performed a perfect Salchow jump. "I thought...you couldn't skate?"

Jamie glided softly to him and flopped her chest against his, wrapping her arms around his neck, "No, I asked you to help me with my skating." Her face lit up and she smiled.

"Oh."

Pushing off from him, Jamie skated lightly backward to a stop and held her arms out, "Oh, come on. Doesn't every young red-blooded Canadian boy have a fantasy about the figure skater in her short skirt?"

Merlin wasn't sure what to say.

Jamie pushed off and did a perfect spin, the short skirt flaring out.

His eyes took in her long legs below the short skirt.

Coming to a stop, Jamie looked at him, "That's it? Nothing?"

Awkward in social situations at the best of times, Merlin couldn't get the words out.

Jamie put her hands on her hips, and shook her head, "You have to work with me here, Dragon." She smiled after a moment, skated to him, grabbed his sleeve and turned him around on his skates. Putting her hands on his buns, she began pushing him toward shore, "C'mon, let's get you off to that armored limousine that will be waiting for you."

"I'm sorry for ruining the outing."

"Outing? This is supposed to be a date."

"Oh, right."

"And yes, I'll take care of Jigs while you're gone. You owe me."

Jigs was Merlin's blue, woolly Chartreux cat and his best buddy, "Thanks, Jaime. I'll repay you—"

"Try coming up with something kinky, Dragon."

"Like me wearing that outfit for you?"

Jamie laughed and squeezed his butt as she pushed.

Chapter 3

M.J. NADON BUILDING, Ottawa

THE TWO-TONE BROWN building was busy. The complex was comprised of seven interconnected buildings over 54 acres. An atrium connected all the buildings at ground level. It housed the Royal Canadian Mounted Police Headquarters as well as National Central Bureau (NCB) for Interpol. It was staffed by thousands of police officers, civilians, public service employees and police officers from Canadian law enforcement agencies and some of its partners such as the Ontario Provincial Police, Sûreté du Québec, and the Service de Police de la Ville de Montréal.

The last time Merlin Dragon was here, he had met with - and was hired by - Director Aubrey Laurent in an empty back office in the Interpol section. Using his Interpol passport to gain unrestricted access, he quickly headed to the Human Resources department. It only dealt with the civilians and public service employees but he was sure they would have access to the directories of every section. He stepped into a front office area of sound deadening carpets, privacy panels, and the hushed whisper of the building's air conditioning.

A tall, middle-aged woman with black glasses on a silver chain, turned on her swivel chair at one of the workstations, "Yes, sir. How may I help you?"

Merlin gave her a half-smile as he approached, "Hi, I'm looking for someone named Powless."

The woman shook her head, "I'm sorry, but we don't have anyone by that name here—"

"No, I mean in the whole building."

Her sculpted eyebrows rose, "I'm sorry, but we don't give out that type of information. And even if I could, you do realize there are thousands of public service employees in this building? I doubt you'll find one Powless."

"Yes, I'm aware of that. But I'm not just talking about the civilian types." He reached into his pocket and handed his passport to her, "I need you to give me a list of everyone with the last name Powless in the entire building."

The woman's hand closed on the passport but her shoulders pulled back, her eyebrows knitting together, "Sir...I think I'm going to—"

"Just put my passport into your system. Please." Merlin hoped that would do the trick.

There was some hesitation, and then the woman turned in her chair, adjusted her glasses, and then used a hand scanner to read the barcode on the passport. She watched the screen for a moment, and ten her eyelashes flickered several times.

Merlin watched her and then asked, "Is everything all right?"

"Uh...yes...Sir." She was clearly flummoxed and looked at the passport, "I mean, Mr. Dragon." She handed the passport to him, "I've just never seen...I've never had anyone in here with your level of clearance. What can I do for you? Oh, yes. Powless, did you say?"

"That's right. If you could give me everyone with that last name, I'll take it from there."

"Uh...yes...uh...give me a minute." She got up and hustled back down a row of cubicles and talked to someone behind a privacy panel. A moment later, a young woman with flaming orange hair peeked around the panel, eying Merlin. Realizing she was being watched, she gave Merlin a sheepish smile and then disappeared again.

Merlin waited as the first woman talked and watched the other woman doing something, occasionally nodding and glancing back at him. He had considered asking for information on Evelyn O'Toole - maybe seeing if they had info on what had happened to her - or where she was - but decided against it. At least, for now. Another thought came to mind as he waited; the faint French accent he heard on the phone call sounded more Parisian than Québécois. Was Evelyn in an ICU unit in France? He ran a hand through his brown hair–

"Sir?"

The woman was standing right there, several pages in hand that she held out, "There are seventeen with the last name Powless."

Flaming orange hair was standing a few feet behind the first.

Merlin took the papers in hand, his eyes running down the list, "Thank you." Her comment suddenly made him wonder if Powless was actually the *first* name of someone. It would be unusual but–

"Is there anything else, sir?"

He was about to ask her to run another search with Powless as a first name when his eyes settled on one line.

"Is there something wrong?"

Merlin scanned the rest of the papers again, then went back to the name that stood out; Constable S. Powless, Interpol Crime Unit. No one else was in Interpol. He pointed at the name, "This one. Can you tell me how to find him?"

The woman turned her body and tilted her head, looking at the line, "Constable S. Powless?"

The orange haired woman came forward, "Sammy?" She turned her head to look, "Yeah, that's Sammy. I see her at lunch sometimes. And at the gym. Nice girl."

"Girl?" Merlin asked.

"Okay, woman."

"No, I mean...."

Orange hair giggled, "Oh, right. Yes, the S is for Samantha but we call her Sammy. That's her extension there behind her name." She turned on her heels, "I'll give her a shout and ask her to come up."

"No, it's fine–"

Wagging her fingers over her shoulder, orange hair said, "It's no problem." She grabbed a phone at the nearest desk and stabbed the buttons in a flash. A moment later, she said, "Hi, Sammy. It's Corrine. Yeah. Listen, there's a Mr. Dragon here looking for you–" She stopped. Raised her eyebrows, and said, "Okay." Setting the phone down, she walked back, giving Merlin a shrug, "Sorry. Sammy said she has something to do first. But she said she can meet you at the Tim Hortons at Banks and Queesdale at three o'clock. That's on the other side of–"

Merlin was on the move, "I know where it is. Thanks."

Chapter 4

TIM HORTONS COFFEE Shop

THIS COFFEE PLACE was on the other side of the Ottawa International Airport and seemed to be a strange place for a meeting. Not that a meeting in a Tim Horton's coffee shop was strange - a lot of people did that. But it was definitely not the closest - he imagined someone working in the Nadon Building would have used the one within walking distance. Then again, this one was surrounded by the Blossom Park, Emerald Woods, and Sawmill Creek neighborhoods. Maybe she lived nearby

The rich smell of coffee, donuts, and pastries teased Merlin's nose as soon as he stepped inside. The place was large, packed and lively with conversation and laughter as well. He slowly moved down the aisle on this side, scanning the crowd for a constable. Or would she be in civilian clothes? He spotted a dark-haired young woman in uniform - a police cap sat on the right side of the table - who looked likely. As he headed in her direction, he noticed her shoulder patch identified her as part of the Bear Island Police Service - which meant she was a member of the Temagami First Nation, an Algonquin Indian band.

She spotted him and gave what seemed to be a subtle nod before her eyes scanned the crowd, and then the parking lot outside the window on her right.

Still not sure if he had the right person, as he reached the table, he bent slightly and said, "Excuse me. Are you–?"

The voice was low but firm as the young woman scanned the crowd again, "Powless, yeah. Grab a coffee and then come back."

Merlin stayed bent over for a brief moment, "Okay–"

"And bring me a large double-double and a honey cruller while you're at it."

Turning on his heels, Merlin went to the other aisle and the lineup where he ordered two of each. Returning with a tray, he set her order in front of her, set his on the other side of the table, and then placed the tray on the nearby tray receptacle/waste bin. He sat down across from the young woman.

The young woman flipped open the tab on the coffee lid, "Sorry for the cloak and dagger stuff, but I wanted to make sure we looked normal, just two people meeting for coffee. Plus, I wanted to make sure you weren't followed and that we aren't being watched."

"Are we?" Merlin flipped open his own tab.

Sipping from the cup, the young woman's dark eyes scanned her surroundings again, "Not that I can see."

"Okay." He sipped and waited.

Powless' eyes settled back on Merlin's face, "You were the same Dragon on Bonaire?"

That startled Merlin. His last assignment - no, the one before - had sent him flying to the Caribbean Island where he had screwed up and gotten arrested. He could feel the heat of embarrassment on his face. And how could she know–?"

Seeing his discomfort, Powless said, "I'm the one who took the call from the Kingdom Representative." She smiled at the words, "It sounded like something from a fairy tale. I passed it on to Director

Laurent. He told me - no, he asked me to keep it under wraps. I was impressed by that. No orders, no...." She shrugged, "It may not sound like much to you but...he treated me with respect. In this profession, that's not something I've had much of as a woman and...as an Indian. You know what I mean?"

"Yes. Well, no, I'm not a woman and I'm not a member of the First Nations so I don't have that experience. But as for the rest, that's been my experience with the Director, he puts his trust in you."

Powless nodded, her eyes focusing internally.

Merlin opened his mouth, intent on asking about Laurent - and Evelyn O'Toole - and he stopped himself.

A moment later, Powless noticed his silence. She nodded subtly, "Right." Her demeanor turned deadly serious, and her eyes scanned the crowd again, "Have you heard the term Novichok?"

"Yes and no. I have no idea what it means."

"Novichok is a Russian word. It means newcomer. It refers to a group of advanced nerve agents developed by the Soviet Union between the early seventies and late nineties."

Merlin's back straightened, "Nerve agents?"

"Right. These are the among the deadliest nerve agents ever made...and it appears one was used on Director Laurent."

His blood running cold, Merlin had to ask, "Is he...?"

"No, he's alive. But Evelyn said they were both in the intensive care unit."

Merlin felt some measure of relief, "That's a bit of good news, at least. It was O'Toole who called me—"

"I figured. I guess she called me because I work for her maintaining the computer systems and databases. She wanted me to contact you...well, she said Mr. Dragon, but I had no idea who or how. She hung up like she was rushed before she could get a lot out. Like she was afraid of something, or someone."

Nodding, Merlin said, "She barely got much out with me before someone took the phone from her. It sounded like she was in Europe, probably France from the accent I heard."

"She is. She and Laurent were at a diplomatic party in Paris. At some place called Les Salons Hoche. I found their itinerary in our system. And I was able to access some French police reports on what happened and where they were taken after the attack. Those early reports were somewhat confusing but it appears O'Toole was conscious and told the investigators she was sure the biological agent was applied by a woman when she mashed an hors-d'oeuvre with shrimp in it on the Directors hand. She said he's allergic to shrimp and she reacted quickly to wipe it anyway."

"Which is how she came into contact with it."

"I think so. There was also a reference that the French government received some kind of intel that said a male was also involved and he was going to finish the job."

Merlin shook his head, "How come I haven't heard anything about this on the news?"

Powless leaned forward, "That's just it. When I tried to find out what was happening, I was told to leave it alone."

"Who told you that?"

"I got a call from Interpol's Secretary-General, Tuur Peeters." Powless put a hand to her chest, "Can you imagine the Secretary-General himself calling *me*?"

"Why would he do that? I don't mean calling you. I mean cover up an attack on someone like this? Especially, one of our own? This should be front page news."

Powless shook her head, "Nope. He said it wasn't his call. He said it's up to the European community." She counted on her fingers, "He said they have the Tour de France bike race that will pass through Italy, Spain, Belgium, and France, of course. It's a big money making event and they don't want to scare tourists away. There's some big soccer tournament taking place not long after. Again, a big money maker. And some big art show - I think he called it Art Basel - it could be affected as well."

"He's putting tourism and economics ahead of a nerve agent attack?"

"I asked the same thing but he repeated it wasn't up to him or Interpol. He was being pressured by two Dutch politicians, and in the end, he said it's up to our political masters. It was their call."

Merlin narrowed his eyes, "It seems I've heard that crap before." He focused internally for a moment, thinking, wondering what he should do - no - what *could* he do?"

Powless slipped her fingers into a top pocket, pulled out a folded paper and slid it across to Merlin, "That's the address of the hospital where they were taken. And that's the name of the doctor treating them."

Taking the paper, Merlin unfolded it, looking at the information, "The Hôtel-Dieu de Paris. Doctor Jean-Baptiste Carbonneau. Okay. What else do you have?"

"That's it—"

Merlin looked up from the paper, "That's it?" He shook his head in confusion, "No offense, but if she had time to tell you all this, why wouldn't she just tell me this herself? Why would she ask me to contact you instead?"

"I have no idea. I presume she figured you could help them physically and I could provide you with whatever information you needed to do that." Leaning forward again, Powless lowered her voice, "But that's just it. We have a problem and I can't."

"What do you mean?"

"After I accessed the information on the computer system, I decided to call a friend who works at NATO Headquarters in Brussels, Belgium. I wanted to check out this Novichok term. That's what I was doing when the Secretary-General called. When I hung up with him,

I went back into the system to look at the reports and print out the information. And...."

"And what?"

"It was gone. All the information was gone. That's why I told you to meet me here. It's like someone was cleaning up and I didn't know who to trust."

Chapter 5

MERLIN CLIMBED THE OPEN AIRSTAIRS and entered the Bombardier Global 8000, the ultra-long-range business jet that was on constant standby for his use as the Stopper. The pilot, Captain Charity Sherrell and the co-pilot, Captain Faith Saab, both members of the Canadian military were waiting for him.

Sherrell gave him a nod of greeting, her face serious, "Welcome back, sir. I'm afraid whatever assignment you're on, the destination hasn't come in yet."

"No. And it won't." Merlin dropped his go-bag on one of the plush seats.

"I don't understand." She gave her partner a glance, "*We* don't understand."

"No, we don't," Saab agreed. "And there's usually a military courier that shows up with material for the secure locker in back...." Her voiced trailed off.

Merlin rubbed the back of his neck and suddenly regretted his lack of thought. He had simply phoned the two pilots and told him he was on the way. He snatched the handles on the go-bag again and headed back to the still open door, "I'm sorry I called you. It was a mistake."

Sherrell's voice was firm, "Mr. Dragon?"

Glancing back over his shoulder, Merlin said, "I'll take a commercial flight. I should have done that in the first place–"

Her voice getting even more serious, Sherrell asked, "Do we need to call Director Laurent to find out what's going on?"

Merlin stopped, one hand on the door frame. He took a deep breath and turned his head, "Director Laurent and his companion, Evelyn O'Toole, were in Paris, France at some function and...they ended up in an Intensive Care Unit, suffering from exposure to a Russian nerve agent."

Sherrell sucked her breath in, "How did that happen?"

"I have no idea." Merlin turned more to look at the two military officers, "And I get the impression someone doesn't want me to know."

Saab eyed him for a moment, then said, "Maybe there's a reason they don't want you to know. Maybe–?"

"I received a call directly from Evelyn O'Toole in her sick bed. So did a Constable Samantha Powless at the Interpol Crime Unit. She works for O'Toole. Powless and I both agree that something is wrong. O'Toole barely had time to tell me to call Powless before someone took the cell phone from her. Powless said O'Toole sounded rushed, like she was afraid someone would overhear when she was told to contact me. Then, when Powless went back into the system after checking out the Russian nerve agent angle, all the reports...including the location on O'Toole and Laurent...they were gone. All gone."

Sherrell looked at Saab, "That doesn't mean anything nefarious is going on."

"I agree," Saab said. She looked at Merlin, "It's possible the files were tasked to the General Directorate for Internal Security in France and access restricted."

Merlin gave her and Sherrell a nod, "I understand. Like I said, I should have gone commercial. There was no need to involve either one of you." He turned and took a step out onto the airstairs.

Sherrell called out, "That doesn't mean we won't take you over there."

"She's right," Saab said, "we just needed to know what was going on. Director Laurent is one of us."

Merlin looked back at them and shook his head, "No, I was wrong to ask. You could get court-marshaled."

"Like she said, Laurent is one of our own," Sherrell told him. "If he's in trouble, we're going to help." She gestured for him to come back inside, "I'll get the plane ready for departure while Saab gets us ready for takeoff."

Stepping back inside, Merlin said, "Are you sure?"

"Yes, sir," Saab said as she took his elbow and directed him to the seats, "buckle in and I'll secure the airstairs,"

"As long as you're sure it won't cause you trouble," Merlin said.

Sherrell walked backward toward the flight deck, "Oh, it will probably cause us trouble big-time. But you're going to owe us big-time as well."

Saab headed to the airstairs, "Yeah. If we're going to take you to Paris, we want you to get us a dancing gig at the Moulin Rouge."

Merlin looked from one pilot to the next, "You're kidding?"

"Nope," Sherrell said, a big grin on her face, "we're ready to go pro and we want to do the Can-Can with those dancers."

Setting his go-bag down, Merlin rubbed his forehead. He had no idea if they were serious or not. Then again, he thought, sometimes people just joked to relieve stress in a tense situation. As he sat down and began to buckle up, he heard the hydraulic whine of the airstairs amid light giggles from Saab - no doubt at his confused and conflicted look.

,

Chapter 6

M.J. NADON BUILDING, Ottawa

CONSTABLE SAMANTHA POWLESS sat hunched over the keyboard inside her cubicle of privacy panels, oblivious to the muted sounds of anyone else in the spacious, open office area. She was determined to figure out what it happened to all that information. She was determined to help Laurent to and O'Toole but she was also concerned as a professional - the Secretary-General be damned if she was going to stand down - her job was to maintain the computer systems and databases and somehow she had failed. Of course, she had to be careful–

"You're looking particularly intense today."

Powless nearly jumped out of her skin.

"Sorry, didn't mean to startle you. I thought you heard me coming up behind you."

Turning in her chair, Powless saw Constable Devan Larkin of the West Vancouver police force. She hadn't even heard him come into her cubicle.

Larkin took a step to the side and stood next to her desk, "I was going down for a coffee and wondered if you were interested in joining me?"

Powless reached out and tapped a key to blank her screen, "Not right now, thanks. I'm busy."

"That's too bad," Larkin said. He picked up her police cap from the side of the desk and rotated it nervously in his hands, "What are you working on? I mean, you're so intense...?"

"Just doing my job, that's how I roll," Powless said. She gave him a smile she wasn't really feeling right now. Larkin had come to work in the building three months ago as a criminal intelligence officer - specializing as a cyber threat analyst and counter-intelligence - and he had shown interest in her, asking her to go for a coffee, a drink or a pizza in various times. She was flattered but right now wasn't a good time to engage in the back and forth.

"All work and no play makes Samantha a dull boy."

Powless raised an eyebrow, "If you think I'm a boy then I'm doing my makeup wrong."

Larkin laughed as he fiddled with her cap, "So much for my trying to be charming."

Leaning forward, Powless reached up and took the cap from him, "You are charming but right now is not a good time. That's all. All play and no work makes Sammy an unemployed police officer." She set the cap n the other side of the desk near the computer screen. "Bring me back a large double-double and and *two* honey crullers and you're back in my good books." She gave him a wink.

Larkin returned a smile, "You got it, *Constable* Powless."

Powless sat back in her chair as he left. The interruption actually made her refocus her attention. Right now she had to help Merlin Dragon and not soothe her bruised ego. Was that it? Was her ego bruised because all that information had disappeared? She shook her head, it didn't matter. What did matter was Evelyn O'Toole and the

Director needed help. Evelyn had reached out to her, had trusted her to supply the support for whatever Dragon needed to do in the field. She set to work, her fingers flying over the keyboard.

Chapter 7

PARIS, FRANCE

IT WAS NEARING 6 p.m. when the Bombardier Global 8000 business jet circled Paris Le Bourget Airport The business aviation-only airport was blessed with a central location that would put Merlin closer to The Hôtel-Dieu de Paris where Laurent and O'Toole lay in ICU. La Ville Lumière - The City of Light - lived up to its name with a variety of colors splashed across the landscape. But Merlin barely noticed - he wondered if they would still be at the hospital.

A light beep sounded and then Sherrell's voice came over the intercom, "We've been cleared to land, sir. Please buckle up."

But Merlin had already been changed and buckled up, ready to land, for some time. Changing from the suit, he now wore a pair a pair of dressy blue jeans and a cotton blend shirt with a turndown collar, untucked and covering his conceal holster in the waistband of the jeans over his back right pocket. The holster held his special, 9mm Beretta PX4 Storm Subcompact handgun. Made from carbon fiber, it could pass through metal detectors without a problem and had Smart Gun technology - the grip had an internal scan of Merlin's palm print and couldn't be fired by anyone else. His 'escape belt' was made of 1.5" nylon webbing, completely non-metallic and was part of the field kit for used by some of Canada's elite forces. The inside of the belt buckle itself held a non-metallic handcuff key and a ceramic razor blade held in place by a Kevlar lanyard. The inside of the belt webbing had dozens of elasticized compartments containing a non-metallic handcuff key, 4.5 feet of Kevlar survival cord, the Escape Stick by Shomer-Tec, a 4-piece, titanium lock-picking kit, and an American Liberty nickel. You turned the nickel to heads-up, slid a fingernail clockwise along the edge and a small blade of hardened stainless steel rotated out. All you had to do was slip it into your pocket and it was doubtful anyone patting you down would be concerned with a small coin - if they even detected it. The dress boots he wore had shoelaces with blacked-brass tips. One tip on each lace was actually a boot-lace handcuff key. Around his wrist, he wore a Pyro-Band bracelet. It had an integral ferrocerium rod that served as a connector as well as a fire source. Rapidly scraping the rod with a sharp edge, such as a knife blade, would send out a shower of sparks to ignite tinder to start a fire. He had also added a Shomer-Tec Carbon Fiber Ventilator to the tools for his job. It was made of ultra-stiff hollow carbon fiber tubing and looked like a standard cheap black pen with a standard pen cap and a pocket clip. But concealed under the cap was a sharp point cut on a bias. The other end was covered with a slightly tacky material to enhance the grip. It was a last-ditch weapon and would be found and removed on a pat-down but he was learning to enhance his chances of survival.

As he watched the darkening terrain below, he reached out and placed a hand on his go-bag, reassuring himself it was still there. It contained his Interpol badge, his credentials, the 999 key - also called a bump key that can be used to open 90% of all cylindrical locks - and several other new items he had gathered in his efforts to increase the tools he could use to fulfill his job as the 'Stopper' - the one Interpol agent tasked with stopping the bad guys by any means necessary.

The Global 8000 bumped to a landing and brought him from his thoughts. As he watched the lights of the terminal, they stayed in the distance as the business jet slowed, took a right turn, taxied for a few moments, and then came to a stop. He unbuckled and stood up. Why were they stopped way out here?

The hydraulic whine of the airstairs beginning to lower was interrupted by a buzzing sound at his belt.

It was his special cell phone, connected to Interpol's I-24/7 secure global police network, allowing him access to the Interpol databases 24 hours a day, 365 days a year. All its other special features were hidden behind facial recognition software, only allowing him access. And only a few people had the number - like Laurent or O'Toole.

Captain Faith Saab appeared, "I'm sorry, sir, We didn't realize–"

Merlin held a finger up as he grabbed his cell phone and answered, hoping, "Yes?"

"It's Constable Powless."

Confused for a moment, Merlin's heart then skipped a beat, afraid of what the call meant, "Did you hear something about them?"

"No. Sorry. I just wanted to touch base with you and fill you in on a few things I've been doing." Her voice went quiet for a moment, like she was looking around to see if anyone was watching or listening. Then she said, "I went into the system and made you a diplomat with full political immunity."

"I appreciate that, but there's a reason why I don't have it–"

"I figured as much. But in this case, I think you need every advantage there is. I'll keep an eye on the system and make sure if someone starts poking around, I can change it. Besides, I remembered you talking about going home and getting your go-bag before heading over. I figured it held your tools of the trade - I have no idea what they are - but if O'Toole is in trouble and asked for you, there's a reason. I presume you have a briefcase or a go-bag?"

"A go-bag."

"Good. Put anything in it you want to hide from prying eyes. It's now considered a diplomatic pouch and won't be subject to a customs search."

Smiling to himself, Merlin appreciated her ingenuity, "Thanks. I was wondering how I was going to explain some things."

"You might still have to go through one of those metal detectors—"

"That won't be a problem."

Powless sounded relieved. "Okay, good."

Captain Saab was standing next to the open door and she took a step back.

A beautiful young woman, in a blue uniform with yellow accents, stepped through the doorway, her smile lighting up the cabin.

Merlin looked the woman over, his eyes narrowing.

"One other thing," Powless said. "Where you're landing, you need to arrange for a van to transport you to the terminal. By effectively making you a diplomat, you should be greeted by a hostess."

"Okay, that explains it. Someone just came onto the plane." He bent at the knees and looked out the side window, " And there's a limousine out there."

"Good. If you need anything, give me a call." She disconnected.

Saab glanced past the young woman, "That's what I was going to say we needed. The tower mentioned it when we landed."

Slipping the phone back on his belt, Merlin felt good knowing someone - in this case, Powless - was able to help in situations like Laurent had done.

The young woman's voice was light and sweet, with a Parisian accent, "You are Mr. Dragon?"

"That's right."

"I am Monique. I am here to escort you to our VIP lounge and to help you through customs." She glanced at Saab, "And his luggage?"

Saab raised an eyebrow, "No luggage, sweetheart. He travels light."

"Light? Ah, yes." Monique turned and stepped outside the cabin, "Follow me, Mr. Dragon, s'il vous plaît."

Merlin headed to the door.

As Merlin passed her, Saab fluttered her eyelashes, "I am Monique."

Merlin suppressed a smile, "Don't you start."

Stepping into the warm night air of Paris, Merlin heard Saab behind him.

"And I am unique. S'il vous plaît"

Merlin shook his head as he clambered down the airstairs and headed for the limousine. It was Monique who held the door open for him. He sat in the back seat as she sat up front with the driver. The drive was quick and Monique politely escorted Merlin to a customs area. As he handed his passport to the customs agent, he asked Monique, "Can you direct me to where I can hire a car?"

Monique held her hand out, "Do you have a credit card, Mr. Dragon?"

Merlin dug into his pocket, "I have a debit card."

"That will do." Monique slipped it from his fingers and walked across the terrazzo floor to a desk with a courtesy telephone.

"Monsieur?"

Realizing it was the customs agent, Merlin said, "Yeah, sorry."

The customs agent eyed the go-bag.

Merlin shook his head, "Diplomatic pouch."

Raising his eyebrows, the customs agent said, "Of course." He eyed the passport again and then his computer screen. Grabbing a stamping tool, he pounded the entry date on the passport and handed it to Merlin, "Welcome to Paris, Mr. Dragon."

"Thank you."

Monique appeared beside him, holding a portable credit card reader. But she looked conflicted.

"What's wrong?"

"Unfortunately...because you have landed after so many have earlier arrivals, I was only able to reserve a....a Lamborghini."

"A Lamborghini?" That was a vehicle that cost a quarter of a million dollars - at a minimum.

"Yes. We have many who come here from the Middle-East and prefer.... All you need to do is enter your PIN number, Mr. Dragon?" The last comment was more question than request.

Taking the reader in hand, Merlin held his breath as he tapped in the PIN. He wondered if the millions of dollars from his last assignment were still on the card. He held the reader out to her as it worked away.

Taking it back, Monique watched the tiny screen. Her face took on a look of delight as a receipt spit it. She handed it and the card to Merlin.

Merlin was suddenly appreciative at the funds he had at his disposal. He glanced at the rental figure before slipping the receipt and card into a pocket. He smiled to himself - wondering what Laurent might say - and that was immediately tempered by where Laurent was and why.

Monique's held a slim arm out and pointed, "Once you pass through the metal detector, turn left and you will see the EuropeCar rental location, They will have your keys. Welcome to France, Mr. Dragon."

Chapter 8

THE HÔTEL-DIEU DE PARIS

MERLIN WAS SOON behind the wheel of an aquamarine blue Lamborghini Aventador S Roadster that had that brand-new car smell. He felt much better driving on the 'wrong side' of the road after his last assignment and the 740 HP motor roared as he followed the GPS navigation directions and pushed the vehicle hard through the streets of Paris. If he got stopped, he'd test out his new 'diplomatic immunity' status.

He was surprised to find a parking spot on a short road that looped around a subway entrance and underground parking just south of the hospital. Parking against the left curb, he double-checked the Beretta, just in case. Slipping it back under his shirt, Merlin then got out and scanned his surroundings. The air was warm and the street was fairly busy with traffic, the horns honking impatiently from time to time. The large square on the right was full of tourists and he understood why. The far side of the square fronted the amazing sight of the soaring, breathtaking façade of Notre-Dame Cathedral. A visit to check it out would be nice but he had no time. Dead ahead was the old, ornate hospital itself. It appeared to cover the entire block. He headed for it, head on a swivel just in case. There was light chatter from the people he passed. Most of them were obviously tourists as well, using their phones or iPads to take pictures of their surroundings, many of them selfies with the buildings as a backdrop. On the other side of the street on the left, a double-decker bus with an open roof and the words *Tour de la ville* painted on the side sat in front of another old cream-colored building. The vehicles coming out of the archway further up the block were police cars. That had to be Préfecture de Police he had noted on the Google map - the cars were coming from a central courtyard.

Cutting across the tree-lined street, he reached the entrance to the Hôtel-Dieu de Paris. It wasn't as grand or opulent as he had expected. The sliding doors opened under the curved archway and he soon found himself in a large open area with gleaming off-white floors. He had expected more people but it was quiet and empty. Two older men in white lab coats and dark trousers were hustling across the floor. Their whispered conversation and light footsteps echoed off the sand-colored walls until they disappeared through a set of swinging doors. A large white and blue information booth stood in the center of the open area. Merlin could see an older woman sitting behind the low counter and he headed for her. The light scent of orange blossoms drifted toward him.

His footsteps alerted her to his approach and the woman removed her rhinestone-trimmed glasses and looked up, "Oui? Comment puis-je vous aider?"

"Do you speak English?" Merlin reached for his passport.

"Yes. How can I help you, monsieur?"

Merlin held the passport out to her, "I'm here to see about a couple of people. Aubrey Laurent and Evelyn O'Toole?"

The woman seemed genuinely puzzled at being handed a passport. But she opened it, looked at it and her eyebrows rose as she looked up at Merlin, "Interpol?"

"Yes. The two people I'm here to see are with Interpol as well. Aubrey Laurent and Evelyn O'Toole. They're supposed to be in your intensive care unit."

Handing the passport back to him, the woman frowned, slipped the fancy glasses on and turned to a computer. Her fingers flew across the keyboard, "Laurent?"

"That's right, Aubrey Laurent." Merlin slipped the passport back into his pocket

She typed away for a moment and then shook her head, "Non, il n'y a personne par ce nom dans l'unité de soins intensifs."

"Pardon?"

"Sorry. There is no one by that name."

"Maybe they were moved to another part of the hospital?"

The woman shook her head, "No, I mean there is no one by that name in the hospital."

"That's impossible. I know they're here."

Shrugging, the woman gestured to the computer, "Je suis désolé, monsieur." She grimaced, "I am sorry. But there is no one by that name in this hospital. Perhaps your Monsieur Laurent is at another hospital?"

Merlin rubbed his forehead. This didn't make any sense. He looked at the woman, "How about Evelyn? Evelyn O'Toole?"

The woman adjusted her glasses as she turned back to the computer and began typing away again, muttering under her breath, "O'Toole, O'Toole, O'Toole." She shook her head after another moment, "Non, monsieur. I am afraid there was no one here by that name as well." She turned to look at Merlin again, "As I have said, perhaps you have the wrong hospital?"

That didn't make any sense. "Were they moved to another hospital? Merlin gestured with his head to her computer, "Can you check to see if they were moved to another hospital?"

The woman took off her glasses, "I am sorry, monsieur, but there is no indication they were *ever* in this hospital. Or that they were moved. I am sorry."

Powless's comment came back to Merlin. The one about someone cleaning up the computer system after she had looked at the files. Was that possible? He took another approach, "Do you have a Doctor Jean-Baptiste Carbonneau here?"

Frowning again at the constant questions, the woman slipped her glasses on and turned to her computer, "Dr. Carbonneau? Yes, I believe so. Ah, yes. Docteur Carbonneau. Étage deux, pièce 204–"

Merlin was on the move, heading for the elevators. His footsteps echoed rapidly off the walls and he pressed the up button a few seconds later. A bell dinged and the doors opened just as the woman called across to him. He ignored whatever she was saying, stepped inside the elevator and pressed the button for the second floor. The doors closed as he stayed only a few inches away from them and the elevator rose smoothly and quickly. He squeezed through the doors as soon as they started opening. The wall signs pointing him to the right, he strode down a plain-beige hallway before they began closing again..Seeing the door he wanted, he rapped on the frosted glass on the upper half and went inside. It was a small room with light green walls, a single desk with a computer, and several filing cabinets.

A man stood at one of the cabinets, a beige file folder in his hand as he was half turned, looking at the person who had barged into his office. "Qui es-tu? Et quelle est la signification de ceci–?"

Merlin saw a man tag with the lettering: J.B. Carbonneau." Doctor Carbonneau? Do you speak English?" He already had his passport out and extended it toward the man.

"Yes, I am Docteur Carbonneau."He took the passport in hand and opened it, "What is this about?"

"As you can see, my name is Merlin Dragon and I'm with Interpol. I'm here about two patients you were treating. Aubrey Laurent and Evelyn O'Toole?"

Carbonneau's eyes definitely registered recognition of the names. But he quickly covered it over and shook his head, closing the passport and extending it to Merlin, "I am sorry. But I don't know anyone by that name."

Merlin took the passport back and slipped it into his pocket, "Which one? Laurent or O'Toole?"

His eyebrows knitting together, Carbonneau said, "I don't know what you mean–?"

"You said you didn't know anyone by that name. Singular. One name. So which name *do* you recognize?"

Looking troubled, Carbonneau shook his head, "No. I think you should leave."

"Or what? Are you going to call the gendarmes? It looks to me like there's a whole building of them across the street."

Hesitating for a moment, Carbonneau then strode over to the desk, reaching for the telephone, "I will call for security–"

Merlin surprised both Carbonneau and himself when he moved quickly and slammed the handset back down on the cradle. Like Saab and Sherrell said: Laurent - and O'Toole - is one of us.

Startled, Carbonneau pulled his hands away from the phone and backed up, hands in the air like it was a robbery, "Please. I don't want any trouble. You must leave."

"I'm not here to cause any trouble. I'm here to–"

The door to the small office flew open and banged back against the wall.

Two men, wearing two-tone blue uniforms, black ties, and a black and gold trimmed kepi on their head, wedged themselves into the doorway. Each held a Glock G43 handgun with a laser sight.

Merlin Dragon looked down at his chest.

Two red laser dots were painted on his shirt.
Right over his heart.

Chapter 9

NOW STANDING with his hands high against the wall in the hallway, legs spread apart, Merlin turned his head as he was searched by one of the officers.

Beyond the other officer still holding his weapon on Merlin, he saw the woman with the rhinestone-trimmed glasses. She was standing down the hallway near the elevators, her arms wrapped around her upper body, hugging herself with trepidation as she watched.

The cell phone was taken first. Patting the back of Merlin's shirt, the officer then lifted it and slid the Beretta out of the holster.

The other officer took the weapon as it was handed to him and he issued an instruction, "Assurez-vous qu'il n'a pas d'autres armes sur lui."

Merlin heard the officer behind him mutter in protest as he continued the search, obviously miffed at being told what to do, "Oui, oui, oui. Tu n'as pas à me le dire."

The officer holding the gun on Merlin turned to look down the hall and gestured for the woman to get back or move away.

Merlin caught sight of the officer's shoulder patch for the first time. It was circular with the words Gendarmerie Nationale on the outside and GIGN on the inside. They were members of the National Gendarmerie Intervention Group, an elite police tactical unit of the French National Gendarmerie. They handled a number of things but two tasks - counter-terrorism, and the surveillance of national threats - fit in with the attack on Laurent and O'Toole.

The gendarme searching him found the Lamborghini's keys and passed them to the other officer. He found the passport next and there was silence for a few moments. The two gendarmes moved a few feet away behind Merlin and began a quiet discussion. A moment later, one of them appeared back to his left, weapon trained on him. The other one stayed behind Merlin and began talking slow but louder, "Vérifiez sur le passeport de Merlin Arthur Dragon, s'il vous plaît. Interpol. Oui." A static sound came across.

Merlin glanced to the gendarme on the left and spotted a tactical handheld radio on his belt. That told him the gendarme behind him was on a police radio, checking him out. That was expected. But something about the call bothered him. His French was poor but he understood enough to know they were checking his passport - then again, it didn't take someone with *any* French to figure that out - but there was just something else that felt off - he just couldn't put a finger on it.

There was silence for a few moments and then more static, followed by some words Merlin couldn't make out.

"Tourne-toi, monsieur, s'il te plaît."

"He doesn't speak French. He's American."

Merlin realized it was Doctor Carbonneau speaking. The man was standing sideways in the doorway to the small office. Merlin put his head down, thinking. The doctor who treated them was reluctant to talk - no, he was scared to talk. The woman at the information desk had no record of Laurent and Evelyn O'Toole. And then two gendarmes from the GIGN showed up - not two security guards - or simply two officers from the Paris Police force. No, it had to be two members of an elite police tactical unit that had military status. Why would they be here if there had been no terrorist-style attack and Laurent or O'Toole were never here–?

"Please turn around, monsieur."

Turning around like he was told, Merlin kept his hands raised.

The searching officer looked at the passport and then at Merlin, "You are with Interpol?"

Merlin merely nodded. And then he decided to push it. Lowering his hand slowly, he held it out, "Yes. And by now you know I have diplomatic immunity. If you don't want an international incident. I'll take my passport back."

The gendarme tapped the passport against his other hand as he smiled. "Yes. Of course."

Standing firmly with his hand out, Merlin saw the smile never reached the gendarme's eyes.

"And why are you in France, Monsieur *Dragon*?"

Merlin noted the emphasis on his name.

The gendarme let out a low breath and shook his head. He pocketed the passport and gestured with his weapon, "Turn around. Hands behind your back."

Merlin stood with his hand out. He glanced to the second gendarme.

Gesturing with his gun as well, the gendarme spoke roughly, "Fais ce qu'il dit. Tourner autour." He pulled a pair of handcuffs from his belt.

Turning and putting his hands behind his back, Merlin tried to make sense of things as he heard the clicking of the handcuffs and felt the metal clamp around his wrists. The diplomatic status didn't work. Why not?

The gendarme took Merlin by the elbow and turned him. A moment later, the second gendarme grabbed Merlin's other elbow and they marched him toward the elevators.

Still standing near the elevators, the woman pressed the down button. Then she backed away down the hallway, her eyes wide, hugging herself again.

The doors began a low rumble as they opened.

Merlin's head dropped and he stumbled.

The gendarme on the left tugged his arm upward, "Hey, hey hey! Qu'est-ce que tu fais?"

The second gendarme grumbled under his breath.

Merlin's head lolled and his steps faltered.

The doors were wide open now.

The light scent of orange blossoms hung on the air.

Placing his hand on the right door, one gendarme kept them open as his partner moved Merlin inside quickly, pushing him face-first against the back of the elevator car. "Stay there," he muttered to Merlin.

The second gendarme stepped inside the car and elevator doors rumbled closed.

Merlin's cheek was against the cold wall and his voice was strained, "I'm not feeling very well."

The gendarme holding him against the back wall moved his head closer, "What are you talking about?"

"I'm not feeling good. I have to sit down." Merlin began sliding down the wall.

"Hey? Ca va?" The gendarme tried to keep Merlin standing but he lost his grip.

The other gendarme moved over to Merlin's left, both of them conversing in French as to what was happening.

Merlin sat on his boots and slumped his head over.

The gendarme on Merlin's left uttered a sound of disgust and took a step back, grumbling in French, "Weak Americans."

Chapter 10

IT WOULD REQUIRE THE SKILLS OF A CONTORTIONIST. Eyes closed and concentrating, Merlin pulled his upper body back slowly - trying to keep his head down like he was out - while trying to push his butt lower. He had to get his fingers on one of the boot-lace handcuff keys. It was his only chance But with his hands cuffed behind his back, it was damn near impossible. His muscles ached and began cramping as his fingers felt for the laces. Arching his back slowly, he pushed his butt lower. A muscle spasm hit his shoulder and he clenched his teeth as he pushed his body harder to get lower. His fingers touched a boot lace. Sliding it between his fingers, the found the tip and pulled. It popped loose. He flipped the key around– the key dropped from his fingers and he nearly panicked before he was able to trap it against his pant leg.

The soft slap of hand against cloth sounded.

A gendarme's voice, "Ca c'était quoi?"

"Quelle?"

The elevator motor whined louder overhead and the car started to settle to a cushioned stop.

Time was running out.

Merlin cautioned himself to move more deliberately. He wouldn't get another chance. Securing the key in his fingers again, he flipped the key around and searched for the keyhole on the cuffs.

The car settled to a stop.

Finally sliding the key into the hole, Merlin held his breath and unlocked the cuffs. The clicking sound was covered by the low rumble of the elevator doors beginning to open.

One of the gendarmes bent over, grabbing Merlin's upper arm and urged him to get up, "Vous devez vous lever–"

Shedding the cuffs, Merlin pulled his arm from the gendarme's grasp, then attacked with an elbow. It collided with the side of the man's neck, striking his carotid artery and jugular vein.

The gendarme pitched forward, stunned.

Merlin's hand grasped the man's shirt and yanked down, banging his head against the back wall. As soon as his body rocked back and dropped to the floor, Merlin spun on his heels, lifting up just enough to clear the torso and he kicked out. There was a crunching sound as he connected with the side of the second gendarme's knee.

Emitting a cry of pain and clutching his knee, the second gendarme keeled over.

Merlin stepped over the torso and threw a punch to the jaw, knocking the second man out. Taking another step, he slammed a palm on the 'close' button. As the doors slid closed, Merlin hit the 'stop' button, leaned over and went to work. Grabbing the second gendarme's cuffs, he made sure he was secure. Then he retrieved the cuffs he had discarded and pulled the other man's arms behind his back, locking his wrists together. Searching the two gendarmes, he found his cell phone, and the Beretta, his keys, and the passport. Then he searched the floor and found the boot-lace handcuff key. No sense letting someone know how he did it–

Static sounded.

Merlin looked to the gendarme lying face down at the back wall of the car.

A muffled voice sounded in the elevator. *"Lefèvre?"*

It was coming from the tactical radio on the gendarme's belt under his body.

"Lefèvre? Êtes-vous là?"

Merlin now knew what it was that bothered him about the gendarme's radio call. And knowing time would be running out, Merlin moved fast, lifting the body and grabbing the tactical radio. Patting the man's pockets, he found his handcuff key. Turning. he found the other man's handcuff key. Stepping over the other body, Merlin's palm hit the 'open' button. The elevator doors emitted a low rumble, sliding open and Merlin stuck his head out as they parted.

The large open area was empty and quiet.

Merlin hit the button for the sixth floor and slammed his palm against the 'close' button. He had one foot between the closing doors when he thought about something else. He slapped the side of one door and they started opening again. Tugging on the second gendarmes clothing, he rolled him a bit one way and then the other until he found his tactical radio as well. Pressing the 'close' button again, he slipped the second radio into a back pocket and stepped through the closing doors. Striding across the gleaming off-white floors, Merlin heard the static from the radio in his hand.

"Lefèvre?"

The voice was clearer now. A Parisian accent, deep in pitch. Definitely a man. But as he had expected, there was nothing 'formal' about the radio call. He had been around enough French in the government areas back home to know the usual jargon on radio calls. When the gendarme radioed in to check out his passport, there was no salutation asking for a specific listener's attention such as 'dispatcher?' or 'headquarters'. There was no 'copy that' - Reçu. 'Over and out' - Terminé. 'Do you read me?' - Est-ce que vous me recevez? Whoever they were communicating with, neither side was going through a normal channel of operation. The gendarmes hadn't been dressed in tactical gear either - which he assumed meant they were trying to stay under the radar. Taking the handcuff keys would make it difficult for anyone to help free them. And taking the radios meant they would have no direct means of communication. Having to use a telephone to make contact with their comrades would give him more time - even if it was only an extra minute or so. But as he approached the main entrance, he realized their contact might be right outside the front entrance, waiting. Maybe there was even a van load of gendarmes in tactical gear as backup. There was no telling what they might do if they realized they were about to lose their prisoner.

Turning to his right, Merlin moved with a sense of urgency, following the signs indicating a 'sortie' or exit in that direction. In moments, he found himself outside in a beautiful gothic courtyard where he cursed under his breath, wondering if was boxing himself in with the move. He kept moving, looking for another 'sortie'. Passing a number of tourists as he crossed the courtyard, moving up and down gothic stairs, he kept his guard up. No one looked like another gendarme but that didn't mean one wasn't operating 'undercover'. He spotted a sign and headed for the door underneath it. He passed through another building into a small courtyard with a dozen vehicles. Beyond a tall, blue double-gate he could hear the noise of traffic and light conversations in a variety of languages. He slipped through the gate to a sidewalk busy with tourists. There was a line of colorful, busy shops across the tree-lined street. He looked to his right - there was the façade of Notre-Dame Cathedral again, facing that open square filled with more tourists. He headed in that direction, now knowing where his car was—

Static. "Barrière?"

It was the other tactical radio.

Pulling the radio from his back pocket as he reached the corner, Merlin got ready to toss both in the trash bin on the other side of the street. He couldn't afford now to have the static attracting attention. He turned his head, checking to the front of the hospital. No gendarmes. No car or van stood out—

Static. Some garbled words.

Merlin raided the radio and listened.

A voice came across the radio, talking slow, making sure his words in Parisian-accented English would be understood. "Mr. Dragon, was it? You are a magician. But I will find you and I will kill you."

Clicking the button, Merlin put the radio to his mouth. He kept his voice low as he blended in with a group or tourists as they started crossing the street, "You're obviously not a team player. You should have said *we* will kill you." Reaching the sidewalk, he dropped the tactical radios in the trash bin before any reply could be made. Weaving his way through the multilingual crowd and across the square, he pulled the Lamborghini's keys from his pocket. He was ten feet away from the edge of the looped road when he stopped dead in his tracks—

Two gendarmes stood - thumbs stuck in their belts and trying to look casual - twenty feet away from the front and the back of the aquamarine blue Lamborghini.

Each wore a black and gold trimmed kepi on their head.

How did the GIGN know that was his car?

Chapter 11

MERLIN WONDERED IF it was a coincidence. He had the Lamborghini's keys in his hand and he pressed the 'lock doors' button on the fob. The car's lights flashed and the horn sounded. The tourists standing or walking nearby barely gave the car a second glance. They simply continued on with their sightseeing.

On the other hand, the two gendarmes immediately went on alert, their hands poised near their weapons as they looked at the car and then scanned the crowd. The gendarme in front of the Lamborghini walked to the car and stood two feet from it, bending and looking to see if anyone was inside. He looked to his partner, shook his head and then shrugged. Scanning the crowd again, he walked back to his earlier position, hooking his thumbs in his belt again and trying to look casual.

It wasn't a coincidence,

Lowering his head but keeping his eyes up, Merlin moved back a few paces behind a group of tourists speaking German. Putting a hand up as if to scratch his forehead, Merlin turned slowly and began walking across the square. Pulling his cell phone, he looked at the screen, opening the hidden features and a secure line. Pressing speed dial with his thumb, he put the phone to his ear. It rang once. He cursed under his breath. There were two GIGN gendarmes on the edge of the tree-lined street on the far side of the hospital where he had come out of that blue gate. That cut off another avenue of escape.

"This is Captain Saab."

"This is Dragon. Have you been approached by anyone from the local police force or the military? Has the tower asked for someone to come onboard?"

"No. I can ask Sherrell—"

"It doesn't matter. I need you to get in the air as soon as possible—"

Saab's voice went on alert, "Why? Do you need help?"

"Long story short, there's nothing you can do right now except get in the air. I have two military gendarmes watching for me to return to the Lamborghini—"

"Why would they—?"

"Their pals tried to arrest me when I asked about our friends - emphasis on tried. How they know that rental ride from the airport is mine is any body's guess—"

"Understood. Where do you want us to go?"

"I'm not sure. Just..." His mind was divided between getting them and the plane out of the reach of the GIGN and getting himself out of a jam. He looked across at the façade of Notre-Dame Cathedral as he gave it some thought, considered going in that direction and maybe going inside. Or maybe going around the building. That might work.

"NATO has an air base near Geilenkirchen, Germany. They have an airstrip that can handle the Global 8000. That puts us out of France and yet close enough to help."

"Perfect. I'll be back in touch." Ending the call, Merlin called up a Google map of the area as he walked, looking for an escape route on the other side of the Cathedral that was out of sight - he came to a stop and cursed again.

The two gendarmes at the far side of the hospital were jogging across the street. heading for the façade of Notre-Dame Cathedral.

He spotted two more gendarmes near the entrance to the hospital. They were standing on the edge of the street with a man in a dark suit.

Merlin looked at the Google map. From what he could tell - they had cut off three directions of escape - and there was a river right behind him. Now what?

Chapter 12

SOMETHING HE HAD noticed when he parked earlier gave him an idea. It was a crazy idea. But it was all he had. Merlin pocketed the phone as he headed back toward the Lamborghini. Pigeons scooted and flapped out of the way as he crossed the square. As he got closer, he glanced at the three in front of the hospital. They were still there, watching. He looked over his shoulder at the other two - he spotted them through the crowd. They were not far from the far edge of the façade now and looking over the tourists. So far, so good.

Merlin blended in back of a crowd of tourists who were listening to a guide who was talking to them about the history of the square and surrounding buildings. From here he could the Lamborghini and the gendarmes off to the left. The road where he had parked took a loop around a subway entrance on the left and an underground parking entrance over on the right. And the concrete island it created between the two streets allowed space to park scooters and motorcycles. He realized he had an additional problem with his solution - every motorcycle or bike he could see was locked with a large chain to an iron post anchored in the cement.

A family of six passed by on his right. They were headed in the direction he needed to go. He slid over to their far side and pulled his cars keys out as he walked with them. He kept his eyes on the two gendarmes standing watch at both ends of the Lamborghini. It exposed him to the ones at the hospital but he had to hope they didn't recognize him from this distance.

As the family approached the street to cross, Merlin pressed the lock button again.

The car's lights flashed and the horn sounded.

Spinning around, the two gendarmes moved in on the car again.

Merlin scooted across the street and headed for the closest bike. It was a two-tone green Kawasaki and looked fast. It also had a massive chain through the back wheel that was threaded through the eye of an iron pipe in the concrete. He looked at the front and shook his head. Wouldn't work for him. Next was a black and gray motorcycle that had a Piaggio label on the side. He hadn't heard of the make but it looked like a crotch-rocket. He looked at the front and discarded it as viable. The same with the next two, a BMW and another Kawasaki. Both unusable.

A grumpy man with deep wrinkles and burnished skin eyed him suspiciously from under a battered Fedora.

Merlin gave him a smile and a nod, continuing on to the next set of bikes. He passed three more bikes and looked over a purple moped with promise. It was an electric start with a kick-start backup and you rode with your feet flat on the floorboard. The chain from the back wheel to the iron pipe in the concrete looked heavier than the bike itself. He pretended to pick up something near the iron pipe while he was actually checking the padlock - it required a key to unlock. Checking the front of the moped, he found the plastic cowl over the ignition was held in place by a single screw. Running a hand over the moped like he was admiring it, Merlin then moved ten feet away to a low concrete wall.

Pretending to look like he was admiring the building across the street, he did his best to discreetly dig into the webbing of his escape belt. Pulling out the Shomer-Tec Escape Stick, he glancing around to see if anyone was watching.

No one was paying any attention to him - except, of course, for the grumpy old guy in the Fedora.

With the feeling time was running out, Merlin went to work peeling off the outer sheath and the end cap of the Escape Stick. He pulled the internal tooth shim pick and slipped it into a back pocket. Putting the rest of the items back in the belt webbing, he then took out his 4-piece, titanium lock-picking kit. Choosing a tension wrench and a pick, he put the rest back in his belt. This was going to be a test of his speed under pressure.

Returning to the moped, he pretended to kneel down by the iron pipe in the concrete to tie a shoelace. He kept his head down and scanned the crowd.

The old man was looking the other way.

Merlin went to work inserting the tension wrench into the bottom of the keyhole on the padlock. Applying slight pressure with it on the bottom of the keyhole, he then inserted the pick at the top of the keyhole and began a lock picking technique called scrubbing, moving it back and forth over the internal pins, trying to find the correct torque and pressure. Seconds passed by that felt more like hours - the lock opened with a click. Slipping it off the chain links, he dropped the padlock to the ground, slipped the tools into a pocket and pulled the chain through the spokes of the back wheel. The metallic rattle and scraping sounded like gunshots, announcing his intentions. That done, he headed for the front of the moped, pulling out the internal tooth shim pick as he glanced around.

The old man was walking over to the gendarme standing to the front of the Lamborghini.

Merlin cursed as he set to work, slipping the end of the shim pick into the screw slot on the front cowl. He had the screw out and the cowl off in seconds but it seemed to take forever. Tossing the cowl and screw to the ground, he now had access to the back of the ignition. He glanced up.

Now talking to the gendarme, the old man was pointing in the direction of the purple moped.

Great. Just great.

Merlin used the serrated edge of the shim pick to saw through the four wires. Slipping the tool into his pocket, Merlin strode to the center of the moped and made sure the kill switch was on as he glanced toward the Lamborghini.

The old man and the gendarme were in an argument. No doubt the old man wanted the officer to check out a suspicious character while the gendarme had a much more important task.

Straddling the moped, Merlin nudged the kickstand up with his heel. Then he drove down on the kickstart pedal.

The moped coughed.

Again.

More coughing and a hiccup.

Merlin glanced over again.

The old man was walking sideways, still pointing and arguing. The real problem was the attention the gendarme walking with him and paying to the motorcycles and mopeds.

A loud voice sounded, "Hé! Qu'est-ce que tu fais?"

Turning his head in the direction of the shout, Merlin saw a young man was in the square across the road. He looked both alarmed and angry. Merlin drove down on the pedal harder.

"Hé! Arrêtez!" The young man began running.

Merlin kicked down harder.

The moped coughed to life and then purred, waiting.

"Arrêtez où vous êtes."

That shout was deeper in tone and came from the direction of the Lamborghini. Merlin saw the gendarme running his way as well.

It was time to go.

Merlin twisted the throttle all the way and the engine's purr changed to a scream. He cranked the wheel hard. Tires squealed and bumped as he accelerated off the concrete island onto the road. He only went twenty feet and a couple of men jumped in front of him, hands out, trying to stop him. He put a foot out and cranked the front wheel hard again. He found himself circling back toward the chasers and he tried to brake - crap! He didn't have any thanks to his engineering work on the wires and he felt the wheels slid sideways. The tires screeched. The engine sputtered and coughed. Putting a foot out on the other side to stay upright, Merlin accelerated, swinging the moped back around. This time he put his head down - both feet flat on the floorboard - and he drove directly for the two who had tried to stop him.

And this time self-preservation kicked in and they jumped out of the way, yelling and shaking their fists.

Merlin turned left to merge into traffic - and then made a decision - he cut right, heading the wrong way up the one-way street.

Vehicles honked and swerved, banging into each other.

Getting killed by a car wasn't good either so he took to the sidewalk. He didn't have a horn so he yelled 'get out of the way' as the engine purred and he fled the scene - topping out at a cool 30 mph.

Chapter 13

MERLIN SAW A CROSS-ROAD up ahead -Quai de la Corse. Beyond that was a bridge over the Seine The traffic was flowing but he only cut his speed to half. He had no idea how soon or how fast those gendarmes would be chasing him and he couldn't wait for a green light. The moped wobbled slightly as he slowed to a crawl at the corner - and then accelerated.

A car barely missed him - the driver leaned on the horn and yelled out his open window in French. A lorry truck came to a screeching stop only inches away. The driver shook his fist and shouted.

People standing on the opposite corner scattered to let the moped through.

Merlin nodded his head as he passed, "Excusez-moi."

A man and a woman stepped back on the sidewalk to allow him through, yelling at him.

He was across the Seine in no time. The traffic on the next street was flowing to the right and he took the sidewalk in that direction, blending in with the traffic as soon as he could. He went a few blocks and spotted a subway entrance on the left. He left the moped mixed in with a number of motorcycles and bicycles before walking to the subway entrance. Turning in a circle, he made sure there were no gendarmes or police cars in sight. Descending into the station, he used his card to withdraw some euros to pay the fare. He had no idea who or what he was up against - and there was a possibility they could track him by the withdrawal - but he would be long gone by that time. The screech of wheels on track told him he had to hurry and he hustled, getting to the platform as the blue and white subway train was pulling in.

It only took a few moments before he was seated and the doors closed.

There were only three other people on the car. Two young people, with backpacks on their lap and earbuds in their ears, sat snapping their fingers and mouthing words to songs only they could hear. The other was a weary-looking woman who sat and stared at the floor.

As the subway train left the station, Merlin pulled his cell phone, connected to Interpol's I-24/7 secure global police network, and hit speed-dial for Constable S. Powless. It took one ring.

"Powless."

"This is Dragon."

"Are you in Paris? Did you find them?"

"No."

"No?"

"No. The woman at the information booth said there wasn't even a record of them ever being in the hospital."

"Powless cursed.

"Is it possible we had the wrong place?"

"No." Powless paused for a moment, "I don't know. The information I saw said they were taken to that hospital. But...."

Merlin rubbed his forehead, "But it's gone and we can't check it."

Powless was silent.

The wheels of the subway clacked away and Merlin rocked slightly.

"I'm sorry. Maybe I was wrong."

"I don't think so," Merlin said. "I tried to talk to that doctor you mentioned. That Carbonneau. But he wouldn't talk, I got the impression he was scared."

"Scared of what?"

"I don't know. Before I could get anything out of him, two gendarmes from the GIGN showed up - that's an elite tactical unit with the French National Gendarmes. They put me in cuffs. I managed to escape but–"

"Why would a tactical unit arrest you at the hospital?"

"I have no idea," Merlin admitted. "They even ignored that diplomatic immunity thing you set up for me."

"They did?" The sound of a keyboard clicking away came across. A few minutes later, Powless spoke again, "Something...something is wrong."

Merlin sat up a bit straighter, "What do you mean wrong? Is the diplomatic status gone?"

"No, you are."

"What?"

"You're not in the system," Powless told him. The clicking sound became more frantic.

Merlin could feel the train beginning to decelerate, slowing down for the next station. The brakes began to squeal. "Sammy? Talk to me?"

"I'm sorry, I can explain it. You're not in the system. Merlin Dragon doesn't show up anywhere."

Feeling the panic starting to rise, Merlin ran a hand through his hair. It wasn't panic for himself - it was the fact someone was cutting off every avenue for him to help Laurent and O'Toole.

There was silence for a few moments and then Powless asked, "What do you want me to do?"

That was a very good question. Merlin wasn't even sure what he was going to do. "Maybe you should just–"

"Stand down? No way. Not while Laurent and O'Toole need our help."

"You sure?'

"Yeah."

"Okay." Merlin still wasn't sure where to go from here. Then a thought struck him, "Check to see if my debit card is still active."

"Your debit card?"

"Yeah. Laurent set one up for my last case."

"Oh. Okay."

Rocking to the right as the train came to a stop, Merlin put a hand on the seat to stay upright and turned his head to see where he was. Pont Neuf station.

No one got on or got off.

Two men stood on the platform. They wore dark blue uniforms and ball caps. The shield on their shirt had the words; Police Nationale. They were standard French police, not the more military gendarmes. But they definitely looked to be on alert. Was it for him? He guesstimated this stop was a few blocks just northwest of the bridge he had crossed. Merlin stopped looking and sat facing the other side of the car, willing the doors to start closing.

"I'm...I'm sorry. I can't tell. I can't see anything connected to you because..."

"Because I don't exist as far as your system is concerned." The doors closed and the subway car began moving again. Merlin considered his next move. Then another thought struck him and he looked at his phone. Something didn't make sense. He talked to Powless again, "Okay. If I'm not in the system, if I'm not part of Interpol anymore, how come my phone still works?"

"I have no idea," Powless admitted. "Termination of employment should entail closing any accounts attached to the individual." Powless was quiet for a moment, then she added, "Course, I'm just guessing."

"You and me both, Powless, you and me both." Merlin looked up at the subway map on the wall. He formed a quick, tentative plan and the next station looked to be the ideal stop to put it into action. But he would have to move fast.

"Are you still there?"

"Yeah, I'm thinking. And no cracks about me being slow."

"I didn't say a thing."

Merlin could detect the slight mirth in her voice at his little joke. It was unintended but it served to lessen the tension in them both. And it brought another mystery to mind. "Can you check French customs?" he asked her.

"French customs?"

"Yeah." He got up and stood next to the doors, holding onto the chrome pole as he rocked back and forth, waiting anxiously for the next station, "Somehow those guys that cuffed me knew I was driving the Lamborghini."

Powless' voice went up an octave, "A Lamborghini? Must be nice."

"It was." The subway train began slowing, the brakes squealing. "We flew into the Paris Le Bourget Airport not that long ago and that's where I picked up the Lamborghini. It was at one of the car rental places in the terminal. I don't remember the name of the rental agency but try and figure out how these guys knew. But don't push it too hard. Try and stay under the radar."

"Will do."

Merlin ended the call as the train pulled to a stop. He didn't see any police or gendarmes this time and as soon as the doors opened, Merlin was on the move into the large crowd on the platform.

Chapter 14

LOUVRE MUSEUM

MERLIN CLIMBED THE STAIRS to the street. It was a busy, noisy area, filled with honking traffic and the multilingual chatter of more tourists. The smells of baked bread and roasted chicken from a number of nearby restaurants was inviting. Off to the left was the amazing sight of the Louvre, the world's largest art museum, and an historic, central landmark. But the sun was beginning to set and he had no time for sight-seeing, let alone taking time to eat a leisurely meal in the middle of an amazing city

He had pulled his cell phone, accessing a Google map. Orienting himself on the corner of Rue de l'Amiral de Coligny and Rue de Rivoli, he spotted the sporting goods store, Intersport Paris Rivoli. Cutting across the street and heading inside, he found an enthusiastic young clerk who spoke good English in the hiking section. Merlin bought a backpack within minutes, fended off a sales pitch about hiking shoes and clothing but bought a cap with the red and blue logo of the Paris Saint-Germain Football Club, and was back on the sidewalk, ready for the next part of his plan. Heading back to the corner, cap pulled low over his eyes, Merlin began using the map on his cell phone to find

ATM machines. It only showed six but as he walked around the blocks, he found more and more. And at each ATM he took out the maximum allowed, 1,500 euros, stuffing it into the backpack. Within an hour, he was back near the Louvre, having found fourteen ATM machines and now had a backpack filled with 21,000 euros. Another ten-minute walk put him inside the Thrifty-Paris Carrousel-Louvre car rental agency. He rented one of the few cars they had left for two days - a red and black Alfa Romeo Giulia premium compact sedan - using the debit card. He had no choice, they wouldn't just take cash - it was a rule the young lady behind the counter said.

That left Merlin with another task as he drove away in the sedan. Several blocks over, he pulled into an underground parking garage. Using the shim pick as a makeshift screwdriver again - he reminded himself to find something better for his belt - he swapped license plates with another car and was on his way again. Several blocks later, he pulled into a parking lot to a bistro and switched plated again.

Twenty minutes later he pulled into a mall that had a Subway sandwich shop. He couldn't order two footlongs with everything- they were called 30-centimeter sandwiches - a useless fact that diverted his mind for a moment - and he bought two anyway and several bottles of an orange drink. Sitting back in the car and eating, he assessed surprise at getting this far. There were no roadblocks or anyone looking for him. At least there didn't appear to be. He was also surprised his access to funds hadn't been cut and he was able to use the ATMs. Or that the police hadn't moved into the blocks where he was pulling cash. What that meant yet, he wasn't sure.

His cell phone rang.

Merlin took his phone in hand and looked at it. In place of the number showing it said 'private caller'.

It rang again.

He answered with one word, "Yeah?"

There was silence for a moment. "Mr. Dragon?"

"Powless?"

The voice sounded relieved, "Yeah. I wondered why you answered that way. Or someone did."

"I just wasn't sure who was calling me."

"I can understand."

Merlin looked at the dashboard clock, "You're still up?"

"Yeah. I was working on what happened to you. I mean in the system."

"Got it. And?"

"I have no idea."

Shaking his head, Merlin said, "You called me to tell me that?"

"No. I've been trying to figure out how someone removed you from the system. Actually, I'm trying to figure out *who* removed you from the system. But so far, no luck. The other thing is, I can't find any record of you having any debit card through Interpol. It looks like Laurent did everything off the books."

Merlin didn't say anything.

There was silence on the other end for a moment as well. Then Powless said, "Aaaaand you don't seem surprised by that. Okay, zip the lip, Sammy. On another note, I was able to get into the French customs database. There is a record of you - through your passport - entering France. And you used your passport as identification - as required - when you rented the car."

Nodding to himself, Merlin said, "And when they did a check of my passport, all of that information popped up."

"Right. There is an indication of someone checking on your passport. And it appears your connection to Interpol was removed by that time so that was all they got."

"Okay, Understood. Does it show who in the National Gendarmerie Intervention Group checked my passport?"

"No," "Powless said. "Which is unusual. Normal protocol is to register who exactly is making the request. Which tells me we're - you

- are dealing with someone in a clandestine position in the French government. Or someone from another government or organization who were able to access the system."

Merlin chewed on his lip, "I'm more inclined to think they were real GIGN."

"Which raises more questions."

"True."

"Can I add one more question?"

"Shoot."

"This advanced nerve agent used on Laurent and O'Toole was developed by the Soviet Union going back to the seventies. Why would the Russians try to kill them? What's in it for them."

Merlin opened his mouth but no words came out. He looked out the window of the Alfa Romeo and across the near-empty dark parking lot.

Powless was silent as well for few moments and then said, "No offense but...I have no idea if your silence means you can't talk about it or—"

"Or if I have no idea. And I don't. I have no idea why the Russians would be involved. Or if they are involved. Or why a group of French tactical gendarmes tried to arrest me. Or where Laurent and O'Toole went - no, I take that back."

Perking up Powless asked, "You know where they are?"

"Sorry, no. I meant I take back that part about the French gendarmes trying to arrest me. Once I was able to get out of their cuffs and out of the hospital, they should have had more men moving in on the area to contain me. They should have sent out an alert to all the police in the surrounding area to pick me up. I escaped on a moped that couldn't get over 30 mph."

"Seriously? That was a slow-motion escape."

"Exactly. They wanted to take me prisoner and stay under the radar while they did it."

"But why?"

"Good question. The thing is we need less questions and more answers."

"Sorry."

"It's fine. I'm just getting frustrated. And angry that we don't have any idea where Laurent and O'Toole are."

"I may have and idea on that."

Merlin sat up straighter, "You do?"

Chapter 15

MERLIN LISTENED and waited for Powless to tell him where he needed to go to rescue Laurent and O'Toole–

"At least I think I know."

A crushing feeling filled Merlin's chest. He sat back and ran both hands through his hair.

"Just hear me out."

His hands on his head, Merlin looked out across the lowly lit parking lot, "I'm listening."

"Yes," Powless agreed. "But I can also hear the sigh in your voice."

"I'll try to do better."

"I would hope so." There was some mirth in her tone. Then she turned serious again, "Sorry, but I'm just trying to keep from cracking up here. To keep us both from cracking up. Okay?"

"Okay. What have you got?"

"I did some research. Nerve agents are the most toxic of the known chemical warfare agents. NATO has a unit called the Biological Chemical Command that coordinates an attack like this in Europe. I called Faith Gerald again - she's the one I was talking to about the term Novichok when the Secretary-General called and everything disappeared in the system. She's part of the military section in Canada's Joint Delegation that works over there with NATO - anyway - Faith was intrigued by my asking about a nerve agent in Europe and she flagged the term in the NATO system because–"

"Can we get to the point?"

"Yes. Mr. Grouchy. The point is there was a NATO call-out for a special helicopter in Europe to transport patients who had been exposed in Paris to a nerve agent–"

Merlin sat up straighter again, "Does she know where it went."

"No. The call-out was gone from the system when Faith checked back in to see if any reports had been filed on the condition of the patients, where they were taken, the details on the hazmat team that would have been called to the location of the–"

Merlin cursed.

"I agree. But get this. Faith says there are only two locations in Europe equipped to handle the patients. There's one in Tours, France, and the other one is in Dublin, Ireland. Tours is the closest, of course. But Dublin is about eight hundred kilometers from Paris, France and just within range of the helicopter. It's a long shot, but–"

Merlin started the Alfa Romeo, "But it's our only shot right now. Send the addresses of both to my phone."

"I will."

"Can you do anything about getting into the computers of both hospitals? See if you can find any indication they're headed there? Maybe they're on a patient list."

"Uh...." Sammy sounded like she was looking around and her voice lowered, "I don't really have that skill set. You know, the *expert* hacker and cracker? Normally, I would turn to a member of the team...."

Merlin felt himself grimace, "And we don't know who we can trust."

"Something like that."

Cursing under his breath, Merlin said, "I'm limited as well. It's like we're flying blind."

"Sorry. I'll keep digging and reaching out to outside people I know I can trust."

"All I can ask is you do your best. The rest is up to me." Ending the call, Merlin put the cell phone in the cup holder and was soon speeding across the parking lot to the street. Reaching the edge of the street, his phone vibrated against the side of the cup holder. He checked it, found both addresses and put the one for Tours into his navigation system. Merlin set the Paris SG cap on the passenger seat, gripped the steering wheel, stomped down on the gas, and took off, "Here I come, guys, no matter what."

Chapter 16

TOURS, FRANCE

IT TOOK FIVE HOURS of driving and Merlin was dead-tired by the time he reached the outskirts of the city located in the center-west of France. It should have only taken three hours but the traffic getting out of Paris was an enormous drain on time and energy. And then it rained halfway down, slowing things again and only stopping twenty minutes ago.

Finally making his way across the Loire River, the navigation system took him to the west, across the city to the Chru Hôpitaux De Tours. He came to a stop on the narrow Boulevard Tonnellé when the navigation system announced; 'Tournez à droite et vous avez atteint votre destination.' He was next to a long white, six-story building. The lights were on but everything was quiet. He pulled ahead and turned right into the entrance road, coming to a stop with the curved front of the building off to the right. As he looked around, he realized he had a problem. Dead ahead and across a parking area, there was another building. And on the other side of the large green space on the left, he saw another building. Leaning over, he took a look at the map on the glowing navigation system. He had to back it out to get an overall picture and his heart sank. He grabbed his cell phone and did a search for the hospital. It was actually a number of buildings that covered an area of almost thirty-seven acres.

Merlin sat back, running his hands over his face. He was tired and now he had a massive area to search through. Rubbing his eyes, he considered how he could set up a search pattern to cover the most ground in the least amount of time. The problem was he had no floor plans for any of the buildings. Finding out where they had been taken in this complex was a monumental task - then something came to mind.

He grabbed his phone and brought up a satellite view of the complex. Zooming in, he began examining the roof of each building, looking for something specific. He found it. A helicopter pad sat on the top of a five-story building that was nestled on the far side of the building on the right and the one dead ahead. It was a good place to start.

Working his way through the interconnecting roads around the buildings, he finally found himself on the road beside the building that had the helicopter landing pad on the roof. Ten feet beyond a two-foot-high stone wall, and a three-foot high steel fence on top of that, he could see half-a-dozen ambulance bays, three of them filled with ambulances parked nose out of the street, ready to go out a moment's notice. Under the light in each empty bay, he could see a roll-up door and a man-door with a keypad. There had to be an easier way in.

He drove ahead and turned right into the road marked Entrée. A few moment later, he pulled off the entry road into a parking area across from the public emergency entrance. Three more ambulances were parked under the soft lights on the oval road to the left of the entrance. On the other side of the glass doors he could see a lobby area. It looked quiet and empty but there would be some night emergency staff on duty at the very least. He could walk in and ask if Laurent or

O'Toole was here but the last time he did that resulted in him being placed in cuffs. He didn't see any evidence of the GIGN but that didn't mean they weren't in there somewhere and waiting. And he didn't see them until too late the last time either. Using his phone to call in would alert them as well.

He had to go in and find them somehow. The front entrance gave him a way in and he wouldn't have to pick any locks - at least not now - but he still had to slip in unnoticed.

Turning off his phone, he slipped it into a pocket, then double-checked his Beretta. He decided this was also a time to add another weapon and he dug out the carbon fiber pen and slipped it into his shirt pocket. Ready to go, he got out and jogged across the street toward the oval road. The air smelled of wet concrete and low clouds scudded across a full moon - the kind that brought out the crazies.

Reaching the first ambulance, the doors were locked as expected. Looking through the side glass, he didn't see anything inside anyway. The back door to the patient compartment was locked as well. No surprise there either.

Glancing to the glass doors to make sure he still wasn't being watched, he made his way to the second ambulance. The door was locked but inside on a hanger on the back wall of the cab, he saw a white jacket with blue lettering on the back; SAMU 37. The door was locked. Merlin noted there was a pull-up type of lock on the door inside. He stepped back, thinking through the training he had gotten from a locksmith back home. Most cars have a double-sided key, so his bump key was useless. Picking the lock might work but would take time, not to mention concentration that meant he might not see someone nearby before it was too late.

Digging into his belt webbing, he pulled out the 4.5 feet of Kevlar survival cord. Next came the American Liberty nickel from his back pocket. He turned the nickel to heads-up, slid a fingernail clockwise along the edge and the small blade of hardened stainless steel rotated out. Not having anything to wedge in between the upper door frame and the black molding around the door frame, Merlin went to work with the blade, cutting out a one-inch section in the rubber molding at the top. The work went quickly. Tying a slip-knot loop on one end of the cord, he slipped it into the gap he'd created and lowered it to the pull-up lock. Between glances around him, he worked to lasso the lock. On the fifth try, he snugged the loop tight around the lock and unlocked the door. Returning everything to its place in his belt webbing, he grabbed the jacket. A cap with the words Service d'Aide Médicale Urgente 37 on it sat on the passenger seat. He grabbed it as well and placed it on his head as he closed the door gently. Donning the jacket, he headed for the front entrance.

Keeping his head down, the ball cap pulled low over his eyes, Merlin entered through the sliding doors into the emergency waiting room filled with two dozen chairs. The heavy scent of antiseptic hung in the air, mingled with blood, sweat and possibly tears from the loved ones who would be waiting out here. In this case, however, just a solitary man sat off to the left, arms crossed, his feet extended and his bucket hat pulled low over his eyes. A women's washroom was off to the left, and the men's washroom off to the right. And dead ahead, on the other side of the waiting area, he could see a wood and glass booth. A young, dark woman with a black-and-gold, braided-twist hairstyle sat behind the glass. She looked to be reading a book and didn't look up at the sound of the doors whispering opening and closing.

The only way he saw into the hospital itself from here were the double doors to the left of the booth - which meant he had to get passed the woman reading the book. He looked to the man with the bucket hat. Then he glanced over his shoulder to the oval road outside.

Was this a trap?

Chapter 17

IN FOR A PENNY, IN FOR A POUND. Or was that in for a one cent euro and a kilogram? This was France after all. Keeping his head down and moving quickly, Merlin did the only thing he could do. Striding across the tile floor, he headed directly for the double doors. His footsteps echoed lightly off the nearly empty room.

The woman turned a page, kept reading.

Almost there.

The woman's head began to lift up, turning to look at him.

Merlin thought about turning around and going back outside. Maybe he could find another way in. No, too late now. Keep going.

Leaning forward slightly, the woman looked at him, "Avez-vous pris mon verre?"

Lifting a hand, Merlin pushed against the right door and he slipped through to the other side, the door flapping closed behind him. Her words had been quick and he wasn't totally sure but it sounded like she had asked him something about a drink. She had mistaken him for someone else. Which was good and bad. If she came after him to see where her drink was, he would be quickly exposed. He kept moving, striding toward a doorway on the far side, passing eight patient bays with open curtains. Only one of the bays was in use with a doctor bandaging the knee of a little girl.

She looked up at Merlin, her hazel eyes filled with tears, "Papa?"

The doctor talked to her in a low, assuring voice as he continued working.

And Merlin kept going.

Reaching the door, he opened it slowly, checking where it went to. On the other side was a junction of three hallways running left, right and straight ahead. Slipping through the doorway, he closed the door softly as he eyed the signs on the wall. The Unité de Soins Intensifs - the ICU - was on the sixth floor and that would be the logical place to start. And hopefully, he could find a computer he could access to find a patient list and location. The elevator was straight ahead and he headed for it, his footsteps echoing lightly off the beige walls. Low voices carried from somewhere further down the hall. As he pressed the up button, two women in light green outfits stepped into the hallway about fifty feet away and headed in his direction.

The wide elevator door began opening with a low rumble.

As Merlin stepped forward, he heard one of the women call out. A moment later, he heard running footsteps. Merlin pressed the button for floor three and then repeatedly pushed on the 'close' button.

The running footsteps came closer.

Merlin held his breath, wondering how he was going to manage a polite conversation in French if they made it in time. Did they have deaf and dumb ambulance drivers?

Another shout. "Attendez!"

The elevator door rumbled closed.

Merlin let out a sigh as he felt the elevator rise under his feet, "Sorry, ladies."

A low whirring sound overhead was the only sound as the car rose floor by floor. The car bumped to a stop and the whirring was silenced.

As the doors rumbled opened, announcing his arrival, Merlin kept his head down but eyes up, arm behind his back in case he needed to pull the Beretta. He stepped halfway out of the elevator, keeping the door open as he checked the green hallway. It was empty in both directions. A glass canopy overhead revealed the silver moon and the dark clouds. It was raining lightly again, the drops bouncing off the glass and running down the curved canopy. The smell of floor cleaner and disinfectant was evident but there was also a sweet smell that seemed familiar. Merlin gave it a moment's thought - he couldn't place it - and he turned his attention to more important matters.

A sign indicated the ICU was off to the left and he headed that way as the elevator rumbled closed behind him. He passed a number of doors with labels like Radiologie, Imagerie Diagnostique, Hématologie and he wondered why he didn't see or hear anyone. Approaching a cross-hallway, the sign on the wall indicated the Unité de Soins Intensifs was somewhere around the corner to the right. Reaching the corner, he peered around to make sure–

The lights went out.

Chapter 18

IN THE SUDDEN DARKNESS, Merlin Dragon froze. He looked up at the glass canopy overhead. It still wasn't raining very hard and he couldn't see rolling thunder-clouds or lightning. Nothing had changed. How could the power just go out? He turned and looked back down the hallway–

There was a curved glint of moonlight one hundred feet away.

Merlin dropped to the floor. His brain told him there was no time to dive.

Muzzle flash and a muffled shot.

The sound of metal puncturing a wall somewhere behind him.

Rolling over, Merlin scooted on his knees around the corner.

Another muffled shot.

The sound of a bullet gouging the vinyl hospital flooring where he had been.

Merlin pulled the Beretta from his conceal holster and sat with his knees up and back against the wall. He listened.

The light patter of rain on the glass canopy overhead.

A whisper of sole over flooring.

Click.

Merlin rolled to his left, stuck his hand around the corner and fired a warning shot,

The explosion echoed off the floor, walls, and glass ceiling.

He pulled back to avoid the expected return fire.

It didn't come.

Merlin rolled to his feet in a crouch, scooted to the other wall and knelt on one knee, back against the wall, weapon up and ready. The shooter should come wide around the corner to get a bead on where he had been.

Silence.

The moonlight softened the darkness as he waited.

Shadows of the raindrops overhead dotted the flooring.

The smell of gunpowder mixed with antiseptic.

Where was the backup power? Every hospital like this had to have emergency standby diesel generators or patients could die in a power outage.

Another thought thudded into his brain and Merlin's blood ran cold. The click he had heard. It was the closing of a door. He looked to the left. The soft outline of another door gave him pause. Was someone moving into one entrance of some room or lab, only to come out another one - and get behind him? It made sense and he moved low toward the outline of the door. Something told him he as wrong. It was a ruse. He swiveled around and moved low back toward the corner–

He collided with a dark figure rushing around the corner to take him by surprise.

They tumbled to the floor.

His Beretta clattered off across the rain patterned flooring into the junction of the hallways. His hat flew off in another direction.

There was the sound of another weapon bouncing off the floor and then a wall.

Merlin grappled with the dark figure - and somehow landed smack on his back. His lungs expelled air.

The dark figure loomed and the moonlight glinted off a fist headed for Merlin's throat - a leopard blow- the first two joints of the fingers folding inward - meant to strike a killing blow with the fore-knuckles.

Instinctively tucking his chin, lifting a shoulder and twisting, Merlin felt the blow glance off his scapula. He rolled back, throwing a fist upward.

There was nothing there but a view of the night sky.

A knee landed against Merlin's lower back and his kidney felt like it exploded. He fought off the paralyzing effect and rolled over, trying to gain some distance and time. He banged against the wall.

The brushing of shoes over flooring.

Looming high against the glass canopy overhead again, the dark figure's arm pulled back in another leopard blow.

Merlin did the only thing he could do in his position against the wall, he clenched his fist and swept his arm out low. It connected with a lower leg.

The dark figure tilted - and then rotated in the air - coming to rest standing up.

Cursing, Merlin realized the figure was standing at a slight angle to him now and he took advantage of the situation. Tucking his arms in, he rolled like a log, taking the feet out from under the attacker.

This time the dark figure landed heavily.

This time Merlin heard a grunt of pain as the attacker's head struck the wall as well. Scrambling around on the floor, Merlin gave himself more distance, looking for his weapon as well. His kidneys hurt and he felt like puking, Spotting the Beretta on the rain-dotted, moonlit floor, he dove for it. Weapon now in both hands, Merlin turned over onto his back. He swept the Beretta back and forth.

Nothing there.

Faint running footsteps.

Merlin swept the Beretta toward each hallway.

The light patter of rain on the glass canopy overhead.

He was alone.

Chapter 19

OTTAWA, CANADA

CONSTABLE SAMANTHA POWLESS let the shower's hot water massage the back of her neck. She had worked long past midnight, digging through the computer system, trying to figure out who had removed Merlin Dragon from the system. And who - and how - someone had removed the information about Director Laurent and Evelyn O'Toole. She had beaten herself up over it several times. Had she imagined it? No, not possible. But where were they–?

The shower curtain exploded inward and wrapped around Powless.

Sammy felt panic strike deep in her chest. Powerful arms took her off her feet and pulled her wrapped body from the shower.

There were metallic snaps and pops as the curtain rings were ripped from the shower rod.

Her wet feet banged over the edge of the tub and slipped across the tile floor of the bathroom. Sammy felt the form of a husky man against her wet body and the bile of fear rose in her throat. A rapist? I'm going to be raped and murdered?

Powerful arms swept the wrapped body around and it slammed into the edge of the open bathroom door.

The blow she took brought back memories of her childhood on the reserve - a drunken father and the violence around her - and that struck Sammy harder than the door itself. That was why she had become a cop. To have her life ended in this way this was like payback for her stupidity of thinking she could get out, that she could make a difference for someone else as a police officer.

The attacker staggered back from the edge of the door, released one arm from around his wrapped victim, growled in anger and slammed the door back against the wall, "Stay open, damn you."

Anger also welled up inside Sammy's breast and she cursed her thinking. She *was* a cop. And she had to *act* like a cop to protect the victim - even if *she* was the victim. She did the only thing she could. Wrapping one leg around the knee of her attacker, she pushed her upper body forward, trying to gain some leverage. He was already off balance from fighting with the door and her efforts paid off.

The attacker's knee buckled and he toppled over, taking Powless with him. But his instincts of self-preservation kicked in and he released his grip around the plastic curtain and his victim to soften his fall.

Sammy grunted as her wrapped body hit the floor. Then she rolled over hard, kicking and lashing out with her arms against the shower curtain, trying to extricate herself from the makeshift prison.

Growling again, the attacker rolled over on the floor and reached for her, grabbing a naked hip, "No you don't sweetheart."

Sammy rolled again and her wet, naked body slipped from his grasp. She grunted in pain again as her back smacked against her small bathroom vanity.

The attacker tried to get up but his foot slipped on the shed water and he fell on his face, cursing.

Sammy rose to her feet, back against the vanity. She knew the man dressed in black - including black gloves - outweighed her by fifty pounds at least and even her police training would be useless in the cramped quarters. She had to resort to street fighting and dirty tactics.

Finally getting his feet under him, the attacker rose up and paused, drinking in the wet, nude body in front of him.

That gave Sammy her chance. She fired an elbow back against the medicine cabinet, shattering the glass. Digging out a long shard with her fingers, she brought it back around in a sweeping motion like a knife.

The attacker was moving forward and then he tried to stop when he realized what she was doing. His feet slipped on the wet tiles and his arms windmilled in a futile attempt to move back. The glass slashed across his chest, opening up a gash in black cloth and pink flesh, and he howled in pain.

Sammy attacked, trying to stab him in the heart.

Slapping her arm to the side, the attacker turned, slipped once more, grabbed the edge of the door to stay upright, and then bolted from the bathroom.

Reacting to her training, Sammy gave chase, yelling, "Stop. Police." The absurdity of it all coursed through her brain. Maybe that should have been 'Stop. Naked police'.

The attacker ran hard down the hallway, skidded to a sideways stop on the parquet flooring, and then took off running across the living room.

Sammy was close behind, yelling, "Stop."

Leaping onto the cushions of the long sofa on the other side of the living room, the attacker looked back as he lifted a foot to step onto the back. His foot caught in the soft material and he pitched over sideways, smashing through the plate glass window and disappearing into the night air outside.

Sliding to a stop in front of the sofa, Sammy looked in shock at the jagged hole in the window. She heard the scream rip through the air- and then it stopped abruptly. Stepping up onto the sofa, Sammy knelt on the back and looked, conscious of the sharp spears of glass around the window frame. The body of the man lay three stories below on the sidewalk. She stepped back onto the floor, her body shaking. She looked down at her hand still holding the makeshift weapon. Blood coated the glass and dripped from her fist. She opened her hand and let the glass knife fall to the parquet flooring. Her hand was cut deeply from the edges of the sharp glass shard but she barely felt the sting.

Sammy felt numb as she turned and headed to her small kitchen. Grabbing the tea towel from the handle of the stove's oven, Sammy wrapped it around her cut hand several times as she walked back into the living area, trying to make sense of what had happened. The sliding glass window on the right side of the long main window was wide open. The screen on the other side was slashed from top to bottom. A rope dangled from the roof two stories above. The attacker had no doubt gotten confused in the chase.

A black backpack sat on the floor. A small cylinder of some type could be seen under the half-open flap. Why would a rapist bring a cylinder to the scene?

Using the end of the towel so as to not contaminate the scene, Sammy folded the flap back and lifted the cylinder out. It was a nitrogen cylinder for carbonating beer. Setting it down, Sammy dug into the backpack and pulled out a clear plastic bag. Next came a plastic tube, a gauge and a roll of duct tape. As she piled the items on the floor, she knew what this was. She'd seen it twice before. It was a helium-hood suicide kit. You put the plastic bag over your head, attached it to the nitrogen cylinder with the tube and you replaced the oxygen in your lungs with the nitrogen. Within five minutes at most, you were gone.

This didn't make any sense.

What she pulled out next only added to the lack of sense. Two sets of plastic cuffs. A small bottle of chloroform, a handkerchief, a vial of sodium thiopental -truth serum - and a needle.

She placed all that on the floor with the other stuff and then stood up, contemplating the items as she wrapped the now blood-stained towel tighter around her palm. A moment later, she realized there was something else on her coffee table to the side. She checked it out. A cloth and a bottle of chloroform. That might be the typical tools of a rapist. But not the other stuff.

Samantha Powless felt an age-old anger rise in her chest. Whatever was intended here - the end result would be a set-up - making it look like she was just another stupid Indian who took her own life.

Chapter 20

TOURS, FRANCE

MERLIN KNEW he had been lucky. As he limped down the dark hallway, hat on his head again, weapon in his right, left hand against his lower back and fighting off the lingering pain and nausea, Merlin definitely knew good fortune had been at his side tonight. His attacker had been more skillful in hand-to-hand fighting. That was a fact. In the soft light, he had seen a fresh blood smear on the wall. Only the head blow against the wall - probably opening a gash over the eyebrow and stunning his opponent - had appeared to be his saving grace. And he had forgotten all about the carbon fiber pen in his pocket - although he wondered if he would have had the time to pull it and...he pushed it from his mind. He still had no idea if Laurent and O'Toole *were* in the ICU. And without power, he had no way of accessing a computer to find their location. But the truth was - he was also in no shape to keep looking right now - he doubted he would survive another attack. Especially if her male partner was around making it two to one. So he did the prudent thing rather than the heroic - he followed the hospital signs on the wall toward the nearest stairwell, cursing under his breath. The whole thing was a damn bust. He had failed them. Again.

Merlin pushed his way into the stairwell - and froze. A moment later, he brought his weapon up and moved to the railing, looking over to the landing below.

Everything was quiet.

He looked back at the bodies. Two men in dark green outfits - probably hospital orderlies - were lying prone in the stairwell. One was slumped in the corner and the other was lying over the top step.

Moving carefully and keeping the gun away from the man in the corner, just in case, Merlin checked his pulse. It was there. And his breathing was steady. He checked the one over the top step. Same thing. Standing back and checking over the railing again, Merlin tried to make sense of the whole thing. Then it struck him. The sweet smelling scent he had detected earlier. It was the gas - the anesthetic called halothane - they had used to knock him out when he had a minor operation a few years ago. Being nervous, he had driven the doctors and nurses crazy asking a lot of questions. He looked up and spotted a ventilation fan. Unless he missed his guess, someone had hooked up the hospital's tanks of the gas to the building's ventilation system. Russian special forces had used a similar gas in the Moscow theater mass hostage crisis some years ago. They had put the gas in the Dubrovka Theater's ventilation system and stormed in. But in this case, the fact there was some activity on the lower floors told him the gas was probably used only on this upper floor. Someone had wanted to move around up here undetected. He swore under his breath again. It was the floor with the ICU. Did that mean Laurent and O'Toole *were* there? But even that didn't make sense. Unless - Merlin felt his blood run cold. Someone had tried to kill Laurent and O'Toole with a nerve agent. Was that same someone here now, trying to finish the job?

Merlin had to fight off the determination to continue his search of the hospital. He had to figuratively regroup and form a more concrete plan. Heading down the stairs, he pulled his cell phone and made a call. It took three flights of stairs before someone answered. Or didn't.

Because - although somebody picked up on the other side - all he could hear was light breathing. "Powless?"

It took a moment and then, "Dragon?"

"Yeah. I'm sorry I'm calling so late - are you okay?"

There was a long slow breath and then, "I'm not sure. I'm naked and I'm wet. And...."

Merlin opened his mouth and closed it as he continued climbing down the stairs.

"Sorry. I guess that sounds like one of those sex hotlines men call."

"I wouldn't know."

"Good answer."

To Merlin, it sounded like Sammy Powless was walking slowly as she talked. And she sounded - shaken? "What's going on? Are you okay?"

She took a few seconds to answer, "Someone just tried to kill me."

Merlin stopped on the stairs, "What? Did you call the police?"

"No, but they'll be here shortly. The guy is lying on the sidewalk below my apartment."

"What? What happened?"

"I'm still not really sure. The guy grabbed me in the shower, wrapped me in the shower curtain and tried to drag me out to the living room. I actually thought he was going to - but he wasn't - anyway...I was able to fight back. I smashed the bathroom mirror to get a weapon and I went after him. He panicked and eventually smashed through the window to the street below."

"Why do you say he wasn't there to...you know?"

Powless was silent for a moment and then she said, "Truthfully, he might've raped me somewhere along the way. But he wasn't here just for that. I found a backpack he brought with him. He had plastic cuffs like you would expect. But he also had a helium-hood suicide kit."

"A what?"

"Long story short, it's a sort of homemade suicide kit that replaces oxygen in your lungs with nitrogen. Kills you in five minutes. He also had a small bottle of chloroform and a handkerchief. But the weird thing is - he also had a vial of sodium thiopental and a needle."

Merlin leaned back against the railing. Truth serum? This didn't make any sense.

"Yeah, I hear you. WTF, right? For some reason, he wanted to...well...I guess interrogate me. Why I don't know. But the thing is... I don't get the feeling he was a professional. You know, someone like a government agent or... I don't know. It just doesn't feel right."

Moving down another flight of stairs, Merlin could hear the confusion in her voice. He understood it because he felt himself.

Powless changed the subject, "Where are you? Did you find O'Toole? Or Laurent?"

"No. I'm in Tours, France. In the hospital here. But I didn't get very far. Someone just tried to kill me."

Swearing under her breath, Powless said, "We're a great pair, aren't we?"

Yeah."

"Was it those French commandos again?" Powless asked. "How did they know you were there?"

Merlin shook his head, "No, it wasn't them." He came to a stop and closed his eyes, thinking. There was something about his attacker - his mind went back to another attack that happened in a house in the dark in Spain.

"What's wrong?"

"It's... it's the person who attacked me. It was dark, but I think it was a woman. I felt...."

"Boobs?"

Merlin couldn't help but smile to himself, "Actually, I was going to say I felt the female form but...yeah." He started moving down the stairs again.

"I'll accept your explanation. Now, why did you call? What did you want me to do? I mean, after I get this all sorted out with the cops?"

As he continued down the stairs, Merlin's mind sifted through what had happened to Sammy. She was right. Something didn't feel right about her attacker. Hell, something didn't seem right about anything since they had gotten the call from O'Toole - like their disappearance - like the GIGN involvement - or the Russian connection—

"Hello? Are you there?"

Still lost in thought and reaching the bottom of the stairs, Merlin first glanced through the glass to the hallway leading into the hospital. No one there. Then he put his hand on the bar of the exit door and looked through the glass to make sure no one was outside, waiting. There was. And they were heading this way from across a narrow street that was lit up.

"Hello–?"

Merlin stepped back quickly as he spoke, "Sammy. I want you to clean the scene there to a certain extent. Leave the plastic cuffs out but hide everything else somewhere. Put it in a closet."

There was alarm in her voice now, "You just called me Sammy. What's wrong?"

"I don't have any time to explain. Make it look like he was there to...you know?" She started to speak but he cut her off, "Once you finish with the cops, I want you to try and figure out who this guy was. Try to figure out why he was there. Figure out where the serum came from. Give me a call later and let me know what you find." He ended the call before she could say any more. There wasn't time. He moved to a trash bin in a corner and quickly deposited his phone, his gun, and the holster. Hurrying back to the stairs, he climbed three steps and lay face down, closing his eyes.

Chapter 21

MERLIN HEARD the exit door open and feet moving with stealth into the area behind him. Boots climbed the stairs and stopped beside him. A hand touched his neck, feeling for a pulse. Then the hand patted him for weapons.

A deep, quiet voice sounded below, Est-il vivant?"

"Oui. il est–"

Merlin groaned and lifted a hand slowly.

"Il est conscient."

Slowly opening his eyes, Merlin feigned fear and drew back, lifting a hand near his head as if he was warding off a bullet or blow.

"Ca va. Ça va. Peux-tu me dire ce qui s'est passé?"

Merlin groaned, closed his eyes and put a hand to his head for a moment. Then he lifted a hand and weakly pointed up the stairs, jabbing it upward a couple of times to indicate someone had gone up there.

"D'accord. Nous y sommes." A hand on his shoulder urged him down the stairs, And then boots passed Merlin.

Turning slightly and lifting his body off the stairs, Merlin saw the two SWAT members climbing upward. Two more SWAT officers entered the exit door, dressed in the standard gear of black tactical uniforms, fire retardant balaclavas to hide their identities, ballistic vests, and Heckler & Koch MP5 9mm submachine guns. The shoulder patch said RAID.

One of the officers put a hand on Merlin's shoulder and then gestured to the door, "Allez, allez, allez."

Knowing that was 'go' and get out, Merlin slowly got up and stumbled down the steps to the side of the door as the two officers moved to the hallway door and moved in tandem inside the hospital. Peering through the glass, Merlin could see a perimeter of officers behind cars across the narrow street. He had to move fast. Retrieving his phone, weapon, and holster and getting them back in place - there was no telling how long before he could get back inside to get them - he then put his hands on his head and pushed his way backward out the door. Spotlights lit him up, casting a hard shadow against a bullseye of light. After a few steps backward - to make sure they saw the blue lettering on the back of his jacket - he then turned and walked slowly across the street with a few weaving steps.

Voices called out and hands beckoned him toward the perimeter.

Moment of truth. Would they search him again or would they assume it had already been done? He had come out within moments of the officers going in.

A hand reached out and grabbed the jacket, pulling Merlin behind a car and then pushed on his back, "Allez." "Allez."

Merlin obliged, moving across the sidewalk to the corner of the building where he sat with his back against the building. He put his head down, pulled his legs in and set his arms on his knees, trying to act like he had been through an ordeal. He stayed that way for several minutes as he listened to the voices, the radios crackling, the coming and going of SWAT members. The lights were trained on the hospital and there were more shadows on this side of the perimeter. He slid over into one of those shadows and oriented himself. He was in a parking area set around a couple of dark buildings. To the right was another two-foot-high stone wall and three-foot-high steel fence combo. A steel gate was wide open, leading to another narrow street. He realized he had gotten disoriented inside and now he wasn't sure if he was on the side or the back of the building.

Looking around again at the controlled chaos, he decided it was time to go. He stood up, brushing his pants off and then headed toward the open gate. Passing through without incident, he crossed the street and began working his way around the building. When he had a chance, he slipped into a dark spot, discarded the coat and cap and then continued on. Finally getting himself oriented, he skirted the outside of the police perimeter and made his way back to his car. The sun was just coming up when he was able to work his way through a back maze of streets in the massive complex and was heading away from the scene.

His body was sore from the tension and adrenalin rush he had gone through. He still had no idea if Laurent or O'Toole was in the hospital. What he did know - he was attacked by an unknown assailant - one who had used a gas to knock out the staff on the upper floor. And who had probably put in a call to SWAT, more than likely to trap him while he - no, *she* escaped.

And then there was Sammy Powless. Attacked by someone who wanted to interrogate her? He had to assume everything was connected.

But *how* was it connected? That was the question.

Chapter 22

MAKING HIS WAY BACK across the Loire River, Merlin drove to a spot south-west of the Tours Val de Loire Airport. Abandoning the Alfa Romeo Giulia in a mall parking lot, the Paris SG cap pulled low over his eyes again, he walked a number of blocks, passing several hotels. until he reached the Hôtel Restaurant La Terrasse Tours Nord. If someone looking for him found the car it gave him a buffer zone and some time if they started a search. The place was nice, with a multilingual staff, a restaurant where he had breakfast, and a nice room. He paid for everything with cash from his backpack. Setting his phone and weapon on the nightstand, he lay back on the bed - the comforter smelled like roses and there were two gold-wrapped chocolates on the pillow beside him - and he closed his eyes for a moment before he took a much-needed shower....

A buzzing and vibrating sounded somewhere in the distance.

Merlin stirred, wondering what it was. He bolted awake, sitting up in the bed. Looking at the clock, he realized he had been sleeping for six hours. The buzzing and vibrating was his own cell phone on the nightstand. He swung his feet off the bed, grabbed the cell phone and answered, his voice groggy, "Yeah?"

"It's Powless. Are you okay? You sound like crap."

"That's good because I feel like crap. What's up?"

"I did like you asked last night. I hid everything but the cuffs. I showed my credentials to the officers who showed up and explained everything. Hell, the scene explained everything. The shower curtains, the rope dangling from the roof... anyway....turns out my feelings were right. This guy wasn't a trained professional. At least not trained by any law enforcement or government agency."

Merlin rubbed a hand over his face. He felt like had just run a marathon. "Any idea who he was?"

"Yeah, the officers who were here did me a professional solid. They called me this morning after they ran his prints and he popped up...I got them right here." The sound of paper rustling carried across the connection. "Guy's name was Robert John Cassler. Known around the area as Bobby the Bouncer."

Realizing he had not only fallen asleep physically but mentally as well, Merlin got off the bed as she talked and headed for the door.

"He got that name because he worked security for a number of the underground clubs around Ottawa and across the River in Gatineau."

"Doesn't sound like the kind of guy who would be carrying around truth serum," Merlin said. He placed his eye against the peep-hole and checked the outside hallway.

"You're right. But half-an-hour ago, I got a call from The Canadian Security Intelligence Service."

Merlin's back straightened, "CSIS? The spy guys? Why?"

"His name was flagged in their database," Powless said. "When they found out his intended victim worked for Interpol, they called to find out what I knew."

Moving back across the room, Merlin passed the foot of the bed and peeked through the curtains, "What did you tell them?"

"Nothing. Literally. Because I don't know anything, right?"

"Right." Merlin stepped back from the curtains and shook his head as he ran a hand through his hair, "So we've still got nothing to help us."

There was a smile that carried across the connection, "Actually, we do. I played my cards right - I guess you could say I played the female card. Told them I was worried. Got a tad hysterical. Some guy that

CSIS is interested in tries to rape me? What if he has friends? What if he–? Anyway, the guy tried to calm me by telling me this Cassler was just trying to move up in the criminal world. Wanted to be a hit man and make big bucks."

"A hit man?"

"Yeah. And apparently, they came across him by accident. He was taped on some phone calls he made to some bikers in Montréal who were under surveillance. The Cobras and the Burnt Jokers have been fighting a gun battle over the drug trade down there for a couple of years. More than a dozen have been killed in their turf war and five of them - four Cobras and one Joker - have been sent to prison on murder charges."

"The Burnt Jokers?"

"What can I tell you? Cassler reached out to the Cobras and then the Jokers, offering his services as a hit man. He reasoned that using an outside gunman would throw the cops off. Neither side went for it."

"I take it they preferred to keep their killing in-house?"

"Something like that. Anyway, Cassler turned to offering his services on the dark web. CSIS maintained surveillance on him because they were afraid some foreign terrorist group might reach out to him. But they say they have no evidence he ever acted as a hit man for anyone. They just figure he saw me at some bar he was working and...well, he just decided to...you know? But the tools he had on him tell us a different story."

"Yeah." Merlin gave it some thought, "So...someone reaches out to him through the dark web...to interrogate you."

"That would be my guess," Powless said. Her voice sounded more subdued as she said, "My guess...grabbing me in the shower...the way he looked at me...the chloroform...he would have eventually raped me - before or after the interrogation - and then did his job as a would-be hit man, making it look like a suicide. Even if they found semen in the autopsy, it wouldn't trigger any red flags. The thing is...a professional would have waited for me to fall asleep before moving in. That would have made his job of controlling me much easier. I'm convinced this guy was adding some thrills to the job and that gave me my one and only chance."

Merlin felt a chill run down his back, "I'm sorry you had to go through that, Sammy. It's partly my fault for involving you–"

"No, Evelyn reached out and *that's* how I'm involved. And I'm glad she did. So don't blame yourself. And deep down, I'm feeling lucky that he *did* add to his job description. It's what saved me. What we really need to focus on is this...why the truth serum? What did I know that he needed to know?"

"Are you working on anything critical in the Nadon Building? Or maybe something from your work with the Bear Island Police Service?"

"Nothing that stands out," Powless said. "I mean...other than working with you on this thing with Laurent and O'Toole, everything's been pretty dull and cut-and-paste. You know what I mean?"

"Yeah."

There was silence on both ends of the call.

Then Merlin made a suggestion, "I know we talked about this before but...maybe you should back away from this–"

"No way," Sammy said. "A cop doesn't back away when the going gets tough. And if they want to get at you through me, fine. They can throw everything at me they want. I'm sticking with it."

"Okay. I hate to say this but...do you think you did something to reveal you were looking through the system to help me?"

"It's possible. I'll just have to try to be more careful. But let's face it, we don't have any other choices, do we?"

Merlin felt himself taking a deep breath and letting it out, "No, not really."

"But here's another question," Sammy said. "So far it looks like the Russians... or someone connected to the Russians...used a Russian nerve agent on two members of Interpol. So far, we don't know why. Correct?"

"Correct."

"Last year we expelled...what was it? Four Russians identified as intelligence officers in the embassy in Ottawa and the consulate general in Montreal?"

"Yeah, something like that. "

"And two years before that we found two deep cover Russian spies living in Canada as a married couple - even had two kids while they were here...?"

"Yeah. What's your point?"

"My point is this - we know the Russians have more embedded assets in-country. Why reach out to some lowlife, bouncer wanna-be hit man? Why not use one of their trained assets who could do a real job at it?"

Merlin rubbed the back of his fingers against his jaw, the day-old - two-day-old? - stubble whispering under his skin, "I would imagine it gives them plausible deniability if he gets caught."

"I could buy that - if it wasn't for the fact the Russians already used a nerve agent that would point back to them in the first place. They had to know that."

"So what are you thinking? We have a rogue Russian agent?"

"I don't know what I'm thinking," Sammy admitted. "But nothing makes sense. Just like everything else since we started looking for Director Laurent and Evelyn O'Toole. Nothing makes sense. Or connects. We have pieces of a puzzle and no picture or edges to work with."

Merlin could hear the anger and frustration and her voice. And he could understand it. He felt the same way himself. Everything he had done to this point had turned out to be a failure. "Okay," he said finally, "right now I'm going to need a shower, something to eat, and maybe a little more shut-eye so I can be effective Not that I'd *been* effective to this point. So how do you want to work this?"

Sammy's voice was tinged with a little more anger now, "Somebody attacked me and probably would've killed me in the end. I'm not gonna take that sitting down. We have a bunch of threads and I'm going to start pulling on them. I'm going to start calling in some favors based on this attack. Somebody else wants to come at me, so be it."

"Okay," Merlin said, "just be careful."

"I'd say somebody else had better be careful."

The call ended.

Chapter 23

AFTER A QUICK SHOWER and a shave with a disposable razor from the front desk, Merlin pulled the Paris SG cap low again and walked two blocks to a small café he had passed last night. He still needed a few more hours of sleep but it was better to keep moving. He had no idea if the police or the attacker was looking for him. Or maybe getting ready to close in on where he was. They were just too many unknowns right now.

The rich scent of coffee and buttery bagels was mouthwatering as he sat down at a small table, set the cap on the table, and ordered. And as he ate, he felt the need for a change of clothing. He had taken an extra pair of socks and underwear in the go-bag when he left the plane but that it been lost when the Lamborghini was surrounded by the gendarmes. And that brought him back to the GIGN. And the Parisian-accented voice of the man he assumed was the leader of the group of gendarmes at the hospital in Paris. *I will find you and I will kill you.* If he and his gendarmes were part of the plot to kill Laurent and O'Toole, he could understand it. That part made sense. But how did the woman who attacked him in the hospital fit in? If she was linked to the GIGN, they would've been the ones to send the SWAT team into the hospital, not the national police force. And that made his thoughts circle back to the GIGN. Why would a French military police force *want* to kill Laurent and O'Toole? Then again, he was only assuming the woman in the hospital here was looking for Laurent and O'Toole like he was. And he was only assuming she wanted to kill them. Was their crossing paths accidental? Merlin shook his head as he popped another piece of succulent bagel into his mouth. There were still too many unknowns–

His cell phone buzzed.

Merlin grabbed it, "Yes?"

"It's Sammy."

Sitting back, Merlin was surprised, "That was fast. One of those threads unraveled?"

"Not really."

Now Merlin felt some depression, "Oh. So what then?"

"I'm at work," Sammy said. "And I decided to go at this like a police investigation. So the first thing I did is I took a notebook and sat in the lunchroom, interrogating myself."

A smile crossed Merlin's face, "Did you play good cop or bad cop?"

There was a smile that came across the call, "Both. I can be a badass witness when I want to be. Had to use a rubber hose on my knee."

"So now you want to interrogate me?"

"Nah," Sammy said. "You're too far away. You're the kind of suspect we often run across that needs water-boarding. Or maybe hanging you from the chains would be better."

"Remind me not to speed when I get home."

"You got it. Anyway, when I went back over my notes, something popped up. Something that bothered me."

"What was it?"

"It had to do with the call I got from the Secretary-General, Tuur Peeters," Sammy said. "Remember I told you when I was trying to find out what was happening he told me to leave it alone?"

"Yeah. That's par for the course for him. What about it?"

"He told me he was getting pressure from a couple of Dutch politicians."

Merlin felt his jaw tighten at the mention of political pressure, "And like it told you before, it's not the first time I've seen this crap. He bows to political pressure whenever necessary."

"Yeah. But why two *Dutch* politicians?"

"What do you mean? The Netherlands is part of Interpol–"

"But two Dutch politicians doesn't make sense," Sammy insisted. "Peeters talked about the Tour de France, and some soccer tournament, and an art festival, and some other stuff, I think. The bike race isn't going through the Netherlands. Peeters didn't say it was and I checked. It isn't. The soccer tournament doesn't have anything to do with that country either- other than playing in it, I guess. And neither does this art thing. I can understand the European Union is supposed to be one big happy family, but why wouldn't he get pressure from some French politicians? Or any of the other countries where it really matters to them economically? I mean, how much does the Netherlands get out of any of these things money wise or in any other way?"

Merlin opened his mouth to explain it away but no words came out. She was right. It didn't make any sense.

Sammy was silent for a moment and then said, "Anyway, I'm still going through my notes and I've reached out to–. Pardon? Hold on."

The call was put on hold and Merlin sat, sipping on his coffee. He gave some thought to Sammy's concern but couldn't see the relevance. Tuur Peeters was a political animal and unconcerned with doing the right thing - it was more concerned with doing the expedient thing - expedient for his career.

Coming back on the line, Sammy said, "Okay, I just got a call back from Faith Gerald. She's the one with CJIRU and the liaison for NATO - anyway - she followed up on that helicopter that we believe took our friends somewhere. There was no official flight plan on record - which is unusual in itself - but she was able to call in a favor of her own and get someone to access the maintenance records."

"How does that help us?"

"Time in service. They have to keep a record from the time the wheels take off to the time they land so they know how long each part, from the fuselage to the props, have been in use."

"I never thought of that," Merlin admitted.

"I guess you just needed a couple of good women in your life."

A weary smile crossed Merlin's face, "Duly noted."

"Anyway," Sammy said, "the time of service was more than enough to carry any patients to Ireland and back."

Merlin reached out and finished his coffee. It went down rich and smooth. He set the empty cup down and stood up, grabbing his backpack, "I guess that means I have a specific destination in mind."

"You want me to call the nearest airport and book a flight for you? That would go faster."

"No–." Merlin was about to say he would call for the Global 8000 business jet but - despite his trust of Sammy herself - he had no idea if someone was listening in. Maybe not on the phone itself - maybe it was a bug on her desk to overhear conversations. It was better to preserve the assets Laurent to had done so much to hide. But there was also something else that scratched at the back of his mind.

"Sorry. I guess I touched a nerve."

Merlin stood on the sidewalk, the sounds of traffic whizzing by, "No, it's not that. I want you to go to a nearby mall and buy yourself a cheap burner phone. Call me when you get it."

Sammy's voice took on a sense of concern, "Why? What's happening? What do you know that I don't know??" It sounded like she was looking around.

"I just think it's time we took this in a different direction."

Chapter 24

CONSTABLE SAMANTHA POWLESS DROVE across the city to Kanata, one of the largest suburbs of Ottawa. She left the highway several times, circling back to make sure no one was following her. Reaching the area's major shopping center, she pulled into Kanata Cellular and bought a cheap disposable phone - a burner phone. Sitting in the Silver Seven Bar and Grill - named after the famed hockey team that dominated the hockey world from 1903 to 1906 - she sat at a table that allowed her to watch the parking lot as well as the highway and called Merlin.

The phone on the other end rang twice and then connected. There was only the light sound of traffic in the background.

"It's Sammy."

"I didn't recognize the number so I wasn't sure," Merlin said.

"Right. I got a burner phone like you said. Now, what's up? You're scaring me. Should I be watching my back?"

"Right now, always," Merlin said. "I just wanted to make sure no one could hear you. Even if we use secure lines inside Interpol, we have no idea if someone higher up can access our conversations."

"You're making me paranoid," Sammy said.

"Doesn't mean they're not out to get you."

"That's an old joke but I get your point. What do you want me to do?"

"Give me the name me for your bank and your account number."

Sammy dug out her wallet and passed the information over, "What do you need that for?"

"I'm going to transfer some money to your account," Merlin told her. "You open a couple more accounts at a couple of different banks when you get time, in case we need to use them. But first, use those funds to buy a dozen burner phones. That way you don't use a debit or credit card that can be tracked. Spread it out over several stores and don't buy anything one behind the other off the rack they put them on. Spread out the serial numbers in case someone is following you. If they can figure out which ones you bought, they could get the phone number from the vendor and track it."

"Sounds like you've done this before."

"Something like that. When we use one of the burners, you dispose of it and go on to the next one."

"Got it."

"Next," Merlin said, "I want you to find me someone who can supply me with a forged passport. See if you can find an ongoing investigation in the Interpol database on a forger in the Paris area. That's where I'm going next. I know there were arrests last year of an organization supplying passports to illegal immigrants coming into France and Belgium–"

"But if it's an ongoing investigation, they might be under surveillance," Sammy warned him.

"I agree. But we need an active forger. Not one already in custody. I'll just have to take my chances. Up to this point, I've just been chasing my tail," Merlin explained, "and we still have no idea where Laurent and O'Toole are. If I head all the way to Ireland–"

"You could be just wasting your time."

"Exactly. Once you find something, give me a call. I'm working on the ATMs in this area to collect more cash in case they - whoever *they* are - can find a way to burn my card. I'll send some money to your account at the next one."

"Okay. You want to tell me what we're doing?" Sammy asked. Her eyes scanned the parking lot and then she turned her head to scan the highway.

"Are you ticklish?"

Sammy blinked, "Uh...yeah. Especially my feet...."

"Then no. You'd be easy to break if they send another person after you."

Opening her mouth, no words came out. Sammy wasn't sure if she should be offended or–

"I'm teasing you. I trust you implicitly. You're a professional and you understand the concept - the less you know the better it is. For now."

The call ended and Sammy looked at the photographs on the wall of the old-time silver seven hockey players. He was right. *That* was a game. What she and Merlin were doing wasn't.

Chapter 25

MERLIN DECIDED TO change things up for his trip back to Paris. He wasn't far from the airport and he took a cab there and grabbed the shuttle to the train station in Saint-Pierre-des-Corps, a town nestled against Tours. He was able to get some more rest as the TGV - Train à Grande Vitesse - France's intercity high-speed rail service zoomed through the beautiful French countryside at 320 km/h. It pulled into Paris Montparnasse Train Station just after sundown. Voices and footsteps echoed off the walls and ceilings as he disembarked with the crowd, jostling with those wanting to get on before they could get out. Dust from the train's breaking pads put a scent similar to burnt paper in the air. His cell phone vibrated and he grabbed it, "Yeah?"

There was the low sound of a voice on the other end of the call.

Merlin spoke a little louder into the phone, "Hold on for a minute. I can't hear you." He hustled through an exit portal and then over to the left, trying to get away from the noisy crowd and the echoes. "Okay, go ahead."

The line went dead

"Crap." Merlin kept the phone in his hand as he strode across the tiled floor to the escalator. As he allowed himself to be carried upward, the cell phone vibrated again. "Hello?"

There was a moment of silence and then a Parisian accent, deep in pitch came across the line, "You were foolish to remain in Paris, Mr. Dragon."

Merlin felt a cold shock run through his veins. It was the same voice he had heard through the tactical radio. The man he had assumed was the leader of the GIGN gendarmes who had tried to arrest him at the hospital. How–?

"You had better perform some of your magic again. Because we are closing in on you. As I told you already once, I will find you and I will kill you–"

Ending the call, Merlin looked down the escalator. He couldn't see any police. He considered trying to push his way back down - or maybe jumping across to the down escalator - and trying to catch a train somewhere. The problem was he had no idea how long it would take before the next one came in. He would be trapped down there.

He looked up. They were now close to the top. His hand drifted towards his back as he considered pulling the Beretta. The family in front of him - the one with the beaming little girl so happy to be here - made him reconsider. He felt his stomach twist in knots. It wasn't right to let innocent people die. And yet, he also had Laurent and O'Toole to think of. He would simply have to find another way to fight his way out of here. He did his best to calm his body, pulled the Paris SG cap low - as if it would hide him - and he got ready for whatever came next.

The escalator shoveled people off the end.

Footsteps echoed loudly.

The crosstalk of voices echoed off the surrounding tiles.

Merlin stepped off the escalator and stopped.

A man behind him bumped into Merlin and muttered something in French as he moved around him.

Two women moved around him, eyes glaring at the rude man who had simply stopped in front of everyone trying to get off the escalator.

Merlin's eyes scanned the crowded station. People moved in all directions. Voices, footsteps, laughter, the sounds of an announcement over a PA system, all of these swirled and echoed around him.

But there were no police.

No gendarmes.

No swat team.

His cell phone buzzed in his hand. Merlin looked at it. Then he answered tentatively, "Yes?"

"You need to dump your cell phone."

It was Sammy. Merlin turned in a circle, still looking for police as he moved behind a concrete pillar, "What's going on, Sammy–?"

"Get yourself a burner phone and call me back. 343-5555. She repeated it and then hung up.

Merlin held the phone as he looked around. This didn't make any sense. Striding across the marble floor to the glass front wall of the station and the exit doors, he stayed alert. Everything looked busy and normal. There was still no indication of a swat team moving in on him. He spotted three security guards dressed in black uniforms with the letters SNCF on the back. SNCF was the French national railway company. Following a terror attack a few years ago, the company had placed thousands of these armed guards on France's trains and around the stations. Merlin felt his body tense up - ready to fight - but these guards were simply walking and watching. They were on alert but definitely not on high alert, looking for him. This didn't make any sense. He knew he kept saying that to himself but it was true. He stopped before he stepped outside and pulled the battery from his phone. He slipped both phone and battery inside the knapsack. Stepping outside to the sidewalk, he turned left, walking with a group of people to stay as hidden as possible. He stopped at the corner, looking in both directions. The street was divided by a walkway lined with trees down the center and an area on both sides for motorcycles. They were parked on both sides as far as the eye could see. He didn't wait for a walk light. He darted across the busy street to the walkway and turned to the left, walking with the crowd, considering whether he should steal another motorcycle and make a slow-motion escape again.

He spotted a gas station not that far ahead on the left. Cutting back across the busy street, he went inside. Sure enough, they had disposable cell phones and he bought a dozen with cash, mixing the makes and serial numbers as much as possible. Moving back across the dark, busy street, barely avoiding the speeding vehicles, Merlin used one of the phones to call Powless.

Someone answered on the other end but stayed silent.

Sitting down on a bench, his backpack beside him, Merlin said, "It's Dragon." His eyes scanned the sidewalks under the streetlights. He watched the headlights as they passed, wondering if one of the vehicles would stop and vomit out a swat team.

Sammy sounded very relieved on the other side, "Man oh man, I need a drink. I wasn't sure I'd get to you in time."

Merlin kept his voice low, "What exactly is happening?"

"Someone put in an ASDL capture filter on my phone at work."

Grabbing his backpack with one hand, Merlin stood up and strolled towards the next bench. It was better to keep moving, just in case, "What exactly are we talking about?"

"It's like an ADSL landline telephone recorder. Only, in that case, it's used to record a telephone conversation without somebody knowing. But the way our phones are set up by our technology experts, the line would beep every five seconds and let me know it's being recorded. What this device does is record the phone numbers coming and going. I never would've seen it if I hadn't dropped one of my gummy bears."

"Gummy bears?"

"Specifically, Trolli's red bear. And don't knock it. It may have saved your life."

"True." Merlin set his backpack on a bench and sat down again, scanning the area around him, "Any idea who did it?"

"No. But I'll work on it. I'm at a Tim Horton's coffee shop. I got the money you sent. And I've gotten you an appointment with a forager in Paris."

"An appointment? Seriously?"

"Yeah. This guy is super cautious but he's supposed to be the best. Which also makes him very expensive."

"I'll find a way to deal with that."

"I hope so," Powless said. "I had to use a back channel to make arrangements through a human smuggler in Libya."

Merlin felt his jaw tighten, "You're sure we're not compromised with your phone being bugged?"

"It's just recording phone numbers, remember? And I used one of the burners," Powless told him. "Anyway, I was given an address. You go there and ask for Charles-Louis Schulmeister."

"Charles-Louis Schulmeister. That's the guy's name?"

"No. I searched the name," Sammy told him. "Turns out the guy was an Austrian double agent for Napoleón Bonaparte."

"Napoleón–? These guys are hilarious."

"What can I tell you. The thing is...if you don't pay once you're in there...you pay. If you know what I mean?"

"Yeah." Merlin continued monitoring the foot and road traffic around him.

"Because we didn't give them much time - we didn't have it - I've got them started on a passport. I was told they have a genuine passport and the documentation for an American reporter from the NY Times."

"How would they get that?"

"Some of this stuff comes from raids or take-overs that rebels or insurgents make on American embassies in foreign countries," Powless explained. "The guy does his magic and he swaps your picture for the reporters when you're there and you're good to go."

"Okay, good work. Send a text with the name and address to this phone. And send me your next phone number once you dispose of the one you're using. I'll return a text message and give you a new number as well. I picked up a dozen on this side."

"Okay."

As soon as the call ended, Merlin was back on the move to the front off the station. There had to be a car rental agency nearby for all the tourists coming and going through this station. As he walked and looked for a sign, he gave some thought to Powless and their move to burner phones on both sides. Under normal circumstances, her suggestion to dump his phone was a good one. But he still wasn't ready yet. Or convinced it was necessary. It felt like someone was trying to screw with him, trying to cut him off from any resources that might help him. Somehow they knew he was in Paris but why weren't they able to track him right to the station? Something wasn't right - and he might need his phones capabilities at some critical point.

He spotted a sign for a Europcar rental location on the far side of the station and before long he was driving away in a Citroën C3 SUV. He changed the plates with a parked car in a nearby mall and was soon on the outskirts of Paris. Now the question was would he make it into the forger's place without being arrested - they might do it on the way out with the goods - and would he get out without being killed if he doesn't have enough money?

Chapter 26

CLICHY-SOUS-BOIS, PARIS

IT TOOK SOME TIME before Merlin was able to make his way to within a block of the address in this commune in the eastern suburbs. Despite being a part of one of the largest cities in Europe, Clichy-sous-Bois was not served by any motorway, major road, or railway. It had become the most isolated and 'notorious' of the inner suburbs of Paris. The population -the vast majority of African heritage- were trapped in unemployment, poverty, and violence.

Parking behind a line of cars, Merlin sat for a moment, looking over the rundown, tightly packed buildings on both sides of the street. The street lamps cast a yellow sepia-like tone over everything and yet spray-painted graffiti in dozens of exploding colors fought their way through. French rap songs shouted from an open second story window across the street. Further down the block, he could see a number of people on both sides of the street. Another strain of music fought against the rap on his left. Behind him, the few people he saw were like shadows skirting the edges of the light. But what he didn't see in either direction was an indication of surveillance on the forger. That didn't mean they weren't there.

Donning his Paris SG cap and grabbing his backpack, Merlin got out, locked the car - he wasn't even sure if that would do any good - and walked along the edge of the cobblestone street to the left of the parked cars instead of on the sidewalk. He wanted to give himself some distance from the buildings. The music became louder as a speaker near the flat roof-line spilled a pulsating, musical mixture of vibrant African and European traditions - Afropean music with African drums, the kora - a West African instrument with 21 strings - saxophones, and electric guitars. Several young men in blue jeans, t-shirts and covered in tattoos, danced on the sidewalk and in the street with attractive young women in cut-offs or tight dresses as others around them smoked or drank from paper bags.

Merlin realized the address was actually a nightclub. The entire front face of the building was a giant spray-painted image of people dancing to music. He slipped between people, heading for the glass front door, the scent of marijuana now heavy in the air.

A shout went up, "Hé, le PSG est le numéro un!"

Two young men were smiling broadly, one of them pointing to his cap and Merlin suddenly felt conspicuous. He traded a high-five - but not the smile - with one of the football fans as he kept moving. Pulling the door open and stepping inside, he found a colorful, noisy atmosphere. People were packed on the dance floor on the far side, a heaving mass under colorful laser lights that blinked and strobed as artificial fog descended from the ceiling. The long, back-lit bar was packed as well. There was no need for surveillance on the outside - it could all be done in here by someone working undercover and blending in with the crowd.

Merlin wondered to this end of the bar and found a barstool against the wall. Setting the backpack at his feet, he pulled a €100 banknote from his pocket.

A young man with slicked-back hair and a black string tie approached him from behind the bar. He set a napkin in front of Merlin, "Oui monsieur. Que puis-je vous obtenir?"

Leaning forward, Merlin looked at the bottles lining the back of the bar as he spoke slowly, "Do you have a cognac?"

"Yes, monsieur. We have Martell Noblige and we have Rémy Martin V. Which would you prefer?"

Merlin was relieved the young man spoke English. The accent was Moroccan but he spoke slow enough to make sure he was understood. "Which one do you recommend?"

The young bartender pursed his lips for a moment, "The Martell is a masculine, elegant Cognac that I am sure you will appreciate."

"Sounds good. Make it a double. With ice."

Giving Merlin a quick nod, the bartender moved away to a workstation and prepared the drink.

Merlin surveyed the crowd around him. There were few tables or stools that were empty. The woman on the stool next to him was turned with her back to him, talking to another young woman. Several young men were standing in a group behind him, drinking, laughing and talking. He turned when he heard a glass clink on the bar in front of him.

"Enjoy, monsieur."

Holding the banknote out to the bartender, Merlin said, "Thank you. Great service. Keep the change."

The young bartender's eyebrows rose in surprised depreciation, "Merci. Thank you."

Taking the drink in hand, Merlin leaned forward, "I was supposed to meet a friend of mine here. Charles-Louis Schulmeister? He said he'd been here a few times and the place was great. Have you seen him? There are so many people in here."

His brow furrowed and the young man shook his head, "Non, monsieur. I am sorry, I don't know the name."

Merlin gave him a shrug and took a sip of his Cognac. As the bartender moved away to another customer at the bar, Merlin turned sideways on his stool and looked over the crowd again. How was he going to find who he was supposed to talk to in here? This didn't make any sense and it was frustrating. How did this forger do business this way? Turning back to his drink, Merlin took another sip, wondering if he should ask a different bartender. An older man was now working this side and the young man who'd served him was now on the far end, serving customers with two other bartenders. Taking off the cap, Merlin ran a hand through his hair, thinking - a hand touched his shoulder and he turned his head–

Warm, full lips pressed against his.

Merlin was frozen in position as a beautiful, mocha face pulled back a few inches.

"You are late, chérie. But I will forgive you."

The woman was beautiful, with sparkling brown eyes and black hair that glistened under the lights. Her French accent was full and teasing and Merlin felt his face burn. He wasn't good in social situations at the best of times, "I think you have the–"

Reaching out and taking his hand, the woman pulled Merlin from the stool, "Come. I want to dance."

Glancing at the bar as he was led through the crowd, Merlin considered simply pulling his hand from hers and getting back to his task at hand. But he didn't want to be rude and create a scene either. The cap was brushed and knocked from his hand and he cursed under his breath as it disappeared under the feet of the crowd behind him. He turned his attention back to the woman, "I think you have the wrong person. Hello?" But the music and the crowd was too loud now for her to hear. He looked down at the long, shapely legs under the short dress and his mind went to Jaimee Hartman. How pissed would she be that his dance lessons were going to be used with someone else? He opened his mouth to call out again when he realized they were actually skirting the dance floor. She led him to an open hallway - a sign on the wall said Privé - and before he could say anything, she pulled him around her to put his back to the hallway.

The woman leaned in and planted her lips on his again.

Merlin's eyes were wide open and he looked at her closed eyes, the long, curling, inviting lashes–

"Do not move or you are dead."

The voice was in Merlin's left ear. And the barrel of a weapon was pressed against his lower back.

But that wasn't the only problem.

Merlin realized he didn't have the backpack with the money either. He had left it back at the bar.

Chapter 27

THE FLOOR UNDER HIS FEET vibrated with the pulsating music as Merlin watched the woman walked away. Her long legs under the short skirt flickered in a robotic-like walk as the colorful laser lights blinked and strobed. He felt his weapon pulled from the conceal holster in back. A moment later, and reached out from behind, grabbed his elbow and turned him around.

Two large men stood several feet away on each side of the hallway. The one on the right had Merlin's weapon stuffed in his belt and he gestured for Merlin to get moving down the hallway.

As he walked past them, they fell in behind him, maintaining a distance that wouldn't allow him to turn and attack them with any efficiency.

"Keep eyes to the front. Go to end of hallway and turn to right."

The accent was French and heavy, the word spoken with authority. Merlin had no idea what was about to happen but he didn't have much choice right now. There was an exit door at the end of the hallway but as soon as he reached it he realized the hallway also kept going on the right and he kept going as instructed. The sound of the pulsing music began to fade into the background. Twenty feet down the hallway, the authoritative voice behind him spoke again.

"Take the door on left."

As he touched the doorknob, Merlin realized the door frame was 14-gauge galvanized steel, which meant the door itself was a heavy, reinforced door. As soon as he stepped inside, he realized why. The room held a passport photo system, a passport printing system, a cutting and laminating system, what looked like a system for creating driver's licenses, several desktop computers and some other equipment he didn't recognize. A long workbench with two stools stood on the right side of the room. Shelves holding paper, several red Jerry cans and other supplies lined the back wall. The air smelled of burnt paper, ink and adhesive.

An old man with white hair and a slight stoop was standing in front of one of the computer monitors and he turned and looked at Merlin. He gestured to a chair next to a table, "Please. Sit."

Merlin did as he was told.

The old man turned back to the computer system without another word.

The two men stood ten feet away from Merlin, watching him.

A moment later, the door opened and closed and the young woman who had kissed Merlin walked by him. She had his backpack in hand. Opening the flap, she dumped all of the money on the table. "There was no other weapon," she said as she dropped the backpack to the floor.

Turning from the monitor, the old man considered the pile of cash. He walked across the floor, picked up a few of the €100 notes from the pile and then looked at Merlin. His accent sounded German, "All of it. Agreed?"

Merlin nodded, "Sounds good."

The old man looked at one of the large men and then gestured to the photo imaging equipment, "Antoine. Take three photographs."

Nodding, Antoine walked over to the equipment, gesturing to Merlin to join him.

As Merlin got up and walked across the floor, he heard the clinking of the woman's heels on the floor as she headed for the reinforced door.

"You are not much of a kisser."

Merlin turned his head and looked at the young woman. He wanted a smart come-back. But no words came out.

The young woman gave him a wry smile and disappeared into the hallway, pulling the door closed behind her.

It only took a few moments for three pictures to be taken and passed to the old man, who then went to work sitting at a stool on the workbench as Merlin sat back in the chair. He watched the old man slip on a headband magnifier with a light, and use a scalpel to work on something on the surface of the bench. Merlin couldn't see what he was doing exactly but the old man moved quickly and efficiently for several minutes, then got up, a shallow box in hand, and walked to the laminating machine. The smell of hot plastic filled the air.

The reinforced door opened and the young woman entered quickly, "La Gendarmerie nationale est là. Une équipe SWAT est dans le bâtiment." She slammed the door shut and the sounds of deadbolts sliding into place rang across the room.

Merlin caught the words *Gendarmerie National* and *SWAT* and his mind whirled. That had to be the GIGN again. How–?

The old man stopped what he was doing and turned to look at Merlin, his face a mask of anger, "Antoine, kill him. Yanis, burn it all."

Antoine stepped forward, pulled a weapon and aimed it at Merlin.

His heart racing and pounding in his ears now, Merlin jumped up from the chair, hands out, "No, no, no, I had nothing to do with that."

The other man, Yanis, already had one of the red Jerry cans in hand and he was sloshing liquid over everything.

The smell of gasoline washed across the room and Merlin knew he only had seconds to live. Antoine was several steps away - how many bullets would he take before he got to the big man? Despite the pounding in his ears, Merlin heard a sliding and turned his head to see the old man and the woman had swung open a section of the shelves at the back, revealing an exit that they slipped through. A whoosh sound caught his attention.

Flames leaped from the gasoline-soaked equipment, beginning to devour everything.

Yanis was already on his way to the escape exit.

Antoine's finger tightened on the trigger.

Chapter 28

AS YANIS REACHED the exit, he put a hand on the edge of the open shelf section and looked back, "Antoine, utilise sa propre arme. Pas de balistique. Essuyez-le et laissez-le." Then he disappeared through the hidden exit.

Antoine nodded without looking away from his target.

Merlin caught the word *balistique*. The suggestion had been to use Merlin's own weapon so the bullets wouldn't track back to these guys. Would the man listen to the advice?

Pulling the Beretta he had confiscated from Merlin, Antoine lowered the other weapon. Without emotion, he raised the Beretta and pulled the trigger. His face flickered in confusion. He pulled the trigger again.

Merlin had his chance. His Beretta had Smart Gun technology - the grip had an internal scan of Merlin's palm print and couldn't be fired by anyone else. Grabbing the chair, he flipped it hard at the man.

Antoine raised his arm to ward off the flying chair.

Taking two quick strides, Merlin kicked the man hard between the legs before he could recover from the double surprise.

Dropping both weapons, Antoine's hands shot between his legs as he pitched forward in pain. His forehead slammed into the floor.

Merlin grabbed his Beretta from the floor, kicked the other weapon away–

Something hard slammed against the other side of the reinforced door. And again.

It sounded like a battering ram was being used and Merlin knew he had only a few moments before they smashed their way inside. He turned on his heels and headed for the exit. Halfway there, he turned around and headed back to the table, doing everything he could to maintain his composure under the mounting pressure. He had placed his own passport, cell phone, several of the burner phones, as well as the debit card inside the zippered pockets of the backpack instead of leaving them in the car. No matter what, he would need them. There was still a job to do as the Stopper. His heart racing, he grabbed the backpack from the floor and began stuffing the money inside. He got most of it, turned and hustled across to the laminating machine. Grabbing everything that the old man had been working on, he stuffed it inside the backpack as well.

The door shuddered now from the pounding. It wouldn't be long before it was breached.

Grabbing the back of Antoine's collar, Merlin dragged him across the floor to the secret exit, pulled him through and then pulled the hidden door closed. He found himself in a narrow, dark passageway between the bones of two walls. Propping the man against the right wall, he tapped him on the shoulder. "I'd start crawling if I were you."

Antoine groaned as he left him behind.

Turned sideways, backpack in one hand and weapon up near his shoulder, Merlin moved down the narrow passageway, looking for another exit out. He found a set of stairs going down instead and he took them slowly, making sure no one was waiting for him. He found a landing and went down another set of stairs. At the bottom, an exit door was still partially open on the right side of the wall. He heard the echoing sound of a car door opening. A voice echoed.

Who was it? And how many?

His heart was still pounding in his ears as Merlin readied himself. Slipping through quickly, he found himself in a concrete garage that could hold a dozen vehicles at least. But there was only one. The old man was thirty feet away, near a black Peugeot SUV, the driver's door wide open. The back door was open and the young woman was bent over, placing something on the back seat. The Peugeot was facing an open roll-door that led to an underground level of a parking garage. A neat getaway route,

Hearing the footsteps as Merlin stepped out onto the concrete floor, the old forger turned swiftly.

Merlin saw the weapon in his hand, coming up to draw a bead centered on his chest.

Lifting his own Beretta, Merlin pulled the trigger.

Both weapons roared and the echo pounded around the garage.

The old man's head snapped back, a bullet hole drilled in his forehead. A moment later, his limp, dead body dropped to the concrete floor with a thud.

The forager's hand had jerked just as he pulled his own trigger and Merlin felt a searing pain on the top of his right shoulder almost an instant before he heard the shot. He dropped the backpack to the floor.

The woman screamed and struggled in the SUV's open back door to get away from the gunfire.

Merlin ignored her - and the pain in his shoulder - as he grit his teeth, picked up the backpack again and strode across the concrete floor. His footsteps echoed as the woman slid along the side of the vehicle towards the back fender, her face a mask of fear. He grunted in pain as he tossed the backpack in the back seat and then slammed the door shut. Glancing into the front of the vehicle, he noted the keys were dangling from the ignition.

Stumbling back from the Peugeot, the woman put her hands up near her face, fearing the worst.

Looking at her, Merlin said, "I should shoot you for that kissing remark but you're probably right." Getting into the vehicle, he placed the Beretta on the dashboard, pulled the door shut and started the vehicle. Pulling slowly into the underground garage, Merlin made sure he didn't see any police or swat team. There were a number of parked cars as he expected, but no flashing lights or automatic weapons trained on him. Following the exit signs and driving up two levels, he soon found himself merging into late-night traffic. It was slow going but he wasn't chased by any police cars or armored vehicles looking to take him down. His hands shook on the steering from the adrenalin rush and he realized how lucky he had been.

Twenty minutes later, he pulled into a mall parking lot, chose a spot away from the splashes of yellow lights, and checked his shoulder. He had been grazed and it hurt like hell, but there was little blood. Grabbing some cash from the backpack, he went into a pharmacy that was still open and grabbed some items to cleanse and bandage the wound as well as a T-shirt. He went back to the car and took care of his shoulder, throwing his shirt to the floor in the back and donning the T-shirt. Then he pulled out the items the old forger had been working on. Was he still good to go? He found an American passport and driver's license with his own picture that looked perfect. The name was Dean Mark Bell. The other item was a N.Y. Times press pass that appeared to be approved by the U.S government. It had a chain to hang the credentials around your neck. The picture wasn't quite square - which meant the forger hadn't quite finished it when the police showed up - but it would serve his purpose. Putting the items back in a zippered pocket, he sat for a few moments, his mind running over and over what had just happened. He grabbed one of the burner phones and punched in a number.

It took a few moments before someone answered on the other side. The voice was sleepy, "Yeah?"

Merlin kept his voice neutral, "You were sleeping?"

"Uh, yeah," Sammy said. It sounded like she was rubbing her face. "It is the middle of the night, you know? Well, more like early morning, I guess. What's up? Did you get what you needed from the forger yet?"

Taking in a deep breath and letting it out slowly, Merlin said, "Yeah. Along with a bullet wound."

"What?" Sammy was now wide awake. "What happened?"

"You tell me. The GIGN showed up. Not the regular police. A military SWAT team. How did they know, Sammy?"

There was silence.

Chapter 29

THE SILENCE SEEMED to go on forever and Merlin waited. His eyes scanned the near-empty parking lot, wondering if more of those Gendarmerie Nationale characters would pop up from somewhere and rush across the dark surface.

Sammy's voice was low and raspy, "Are you accusing me of something?"

"I don't know. You tell me. If we're using burner phones on both sides...how did they know I was there?"

The voice became harsher, "I told you the place would be under surveillance. You wanted someone who was actively forging documents. Remember?"

Merlin's voice rose as well, "That's a standard criminal investigation for a standard police force. Not for a military-style force that concentrates on terrorism and counterintelligence."

"So maybe this happens to be one of those times when you need someone in terrorism and counterintelligence?" Sammy shot back. "Terrorists can use false documents as well, you know?"

Opening and closing his mouth, Merlin's jaw tensed. What she said was true. Was it all a coincidence?

Sammy was silent for a moment and then she said, "Yeah, I don't believe in coincidences either."

Merlin sat back, raised his head and closed his eyes, "What the...was going on?

The only thing on either side of the call for a few moments was breathing. It was Sammy who spoke first, "Maybe someone is watching everything I do on the computer at work. I mean... I found that telephone recorder but...."

His voice rose again and Merlin insisted, "You can't assume there's not another device. Or maybe....I don't know...maybe software like a keystroke logger on your computer."

"No, it's not possible. Our systems are constantly monitored for–"

"We have no idea who we're up against," Merlin reminded her. "It could be anyone in Interpol."

A sigh-like sound came across the phone, "You're right. But being able to do something like that would require a massive conspiracy. There would have to be a lot of people involved. I guess it's possible but...."

"But it's not probable. So how then?"

"I wish I knew. I wish I could give you an answer." Sammy slipped into silence again. "Look," she said finally, "all I can do is ask you to trust me. I know you don't know me, but–"

"But Evelyn O'Toole did. She trusted you enough to call you. She trusted you enough to put us together."

"But you're still not sure."

"Can you blame me?" Merlin asked.

"No, not really." Sammy cursed, "Somebody is trying to screw with us."

Merlin used the heels of his hands to rub his eyes, "Or they have another agenda. One we can't see."

The two lapsed into silence again, both thinking. Finally, Sammy said, "What do you want me to do?"

Looking out across the parking lot, Merlin wasn't sure.

"Okay look, I'm going to do everything I can to figure this out. You do whatever you need to do. But *don't* tell me what you're going to do. Not right now. You know what I mean?"

"Yeah." Merlin chewed on his lip, "The problem is, I think this is what somebody wanted."

"I agree. But what choice do we have?"

"None. Not right now. I'll send you a text with my next burner phone number." Merlin ended the call, grabbed a second burner, entered the number and sent a text. Driving across the parking lot, he lowered the window and dropped the burner phone he had been using in a trashcan. Driving to the exit, he sat there for a few moments, thinking. Sammy was right. Every idea - every plan that came to him right now - was mulled over and rejected. Somebody *was* screwing with them, sowing confusion in the ranks, as it were. Or maybe he was right. Maybe there was just another agenda. The question was - what was it? One thing was sure, he needed rest more than anything right now. He used the navigation system to find a hotel and he found a viable option an hour north on the A1 highway. It took close to two hours before he was finally able to lay his head down on a pillow next to two more chocolates wrapped in gold foil. Sleep didn't come easy.

Chapter 30

M.J. NADON BUILDING, Ottawa

CONSTABLE SAMANTHA POWLESS sat inside her cubicle of privacy panels, staring at her computer's screen. The screen saver image of a tropical beach stared back at her. She'd come in early, before anyone else, determined to figure out how someone knew everything she was doing - everything *they* were doing - she was in this *with* Merlin Dragon, after all. Instead, she had sat there, like a lump, afraid to do anything. No, not afraid. Concerned. Concerned that whatever she did next would result in a catastrophe. Maybe even the death of O'Toole and/or the Director. And maybe even Merlin Dragon. Cursing her own lack of action, Sammy stood up, grabbed her police hat and stepped outside her cubicle.

The spacious, open office was beginning to hum with activity now. Constable Devan Larkin - the handsome young man of the West Vancouver police force - the one who had caught her interest the first day he arrived - was standing near his own cubicle and workstation. He was talking to Amanda Colson - the one with the shiny hair and white teeth and...that body. The one that Sammy assumed was sculpted by long hours in the gym - had to be - who would be that cruel to give

Sammy a body that was trim and athletic but not sculpted–? Sammy chastised herself. Talking to yourself using your own name in the third person was...what? It didn't matter. She was acting jealous and - that didn't matter either. She was trying to distract herself from the task at hand. The one she had no handle on. And the one that said she should get the handsome Mr. Larkin involved. His expertise might just crack the–

Constable Devan Larkin glanced in her direction, saw her, raised a hand in hello and smiled.

Amanda Colson looked over to see who he was signaling to. Spotting Sammy, Amanda smiled and wiggled fingers of hello in her direction as well.

Sammy flashed a smile in their direction. No, not a smile, more a grimace. Crap. Colson will think I'm jealous or something. She swung around on her heels, slapped the hat on her head and headed for the elevator. Light running footsteps sounded behind here just as she pressed the down button.

"Good morning, Constable Powless."

Tugging at her ear, Sammy glanced at Larkin, "Morning." She pressed the button again. And again.

"It won't come any faster."

"So I hear." Sammy pressed it again.

"Are we going for a coffee? I'm buying." Larkin held up two fingers, "And a couple of honey crullers, your favorite. That should seal the deal."

Sammy smiled at him but it was more a grimace again, "Sorry, I can't. Duty calls."

Larkin narrowed his eyes at her and then glanced at her hat, "Okay. I understand. If there's anything I can do...?"

The elevator doors whispered open and Sammy stepped forward, stabbing the button for the main floor, "Thanks for the offer. But I'm fine." She pressed the closed door button, waiting awkwardly for the doors to begin whispering closed.

The handsome young Constable just stood there looking at her.

Just before the doors closed, Sammy said, "Thanks for the offer of coffee. And the honey crullers."

"Of course."

Sammy chastised herself again as the elevator car dropped towards the main floor. *You're going to lose your chance, girl.* The doors were barely open before Sammy was striding across the atrium floor to the front doors. The noise and voices of the crowd around her barely registered. She was on a mission.

An hour-and-a-half later, she sat in the far corner of a Tim Horton's coffee shop, hat on the table, a large double-double coffee at her elbow and a new laptop in front of her. Inserting a thumb drive, over the next two hours she set up hacking, cracking, and masking programs, much of it software that had been confiscated from criminal hackers, and in many cases improved by computer experts around her at work for use as counter-intelligence tools. She never suspected she would be using it against someone withing Interpol. *If* they were inside Interpol she reminded herself. She still wanted to believe the good guys were good guys.

Now that she was set, the first thing she did was use software to hide the IP address she would be using through the coffee shop's WIFI connection, she typed in the personal email address for Faith Gerald at NATO Headquarters in Brussels, Belgium from memory and sent a message: Need to talk. Call +1-613-555-0147 ASAP. Sammy. That done, she set the burner phone on the table next to the laptop, picked up her coffee and sat back for a reply or a phone call. She sipped her coffee. And waited. And waited. She checked the clock. Brussels was 6 hours ahead of Ottawa, which meant Faith wasn't working. She knew that for a fact. She also knew Faith usually wasn't far from her tablet - reading, television, social media, music - she used it for everything.

She didn't even have a real television, and she had a speaker dock for the tablet instead of a stereo system. Something wasn't right. Sammy calmed yourself. Maybe she was on the date - although she had said her job didn't allow much time for social activity like a date. Instead of waiting to talk to Faith first, she bent forward, placed her hands on the keyboard and decided to try and log into the Interpol system—

The burner phone buzzed and rattled on the table.

Grabbing it with urgency Sammy kept her voice low, "Hello?"

"Sammy?"

Relief filtered through Sammy, "Yeah. I was getting worried, Faith. It's not like you to−"

"I had to go and buy a disposable phone first."

Now a fear filtered through Sammy, "A burner phone? Why?" What happened−?"

"You tell me," Faith insisted. "You're not using your personal phone either. And don't give me any crap about just getting a new phone. What's going on?"

Sammy was silent. This wasn't like her friend. She glanced out the window, trying to figure out what was going on here, Trying to buy some time−

"Come on Sammy. Talk to me. This is your friend, Faith. What are you into?"

"I'm not sure what you mean?" Sammy was about to hang up, to tell her to just forget about it−

"The Ambassador to NATO came to me, Sammy. He knew about the Novichok conversation. Or at least that we had talked about it. Wanted to know what else we had been talking about. *Someone* knew we talked, Sammy."

Chapter 31

SAMMY POWLESS NOW FELT a chill run through her. How did they know? None of this made any sense. She scanned the noisy crowd, looking for evidence she was being watched. No, it was more than being watched. They were listening. But how? She was using burner phones - she had a brand-new laptop–

Faith Gerald broke into her frantic thoughts, "You're not even going to talk to me?"

Sammy swallowed, almost afraid to say a single word, "What...what did you tell the Ambassador?"

"Come on, Sammy. You know me better than that." Faith sounded hurt.

Sammy closed the laptop with her other hand, looking around again, "Look. It's probably better if you don't–"

"And don't say that. We're friends. Friends help friends."

"In this situation, a friend wouldn't let you get involved."

"But you did. Which means you need my help. Which means a lot to me," Faith insisted.

Sammy hesitated. And then she slapped the hat on her head, picked up the laptop and carried it in one hand as she headed for the exit, "Hold on." Striding across the parking lot, watching every car parked or driving around her, Sammy headed for the grass strip beyond the curb at the back and a sparse stretch of trees beyond that. She didn't want to be in the coffee shop or her car or - she turned in a circle as she walked, looking for someone with a parabolic listening device. Reaching the grass, she set the laptop on the curb. Scanning the trees for anyone that might be there, she began to explain the situation. At one point, she strode to the large metal dumpster sitting fifteen feet away on the pavement at the edge of the curb, peeking in, making sure someone wasn't hiding there. *Paranoid much?*

When Sammy finally finished, Faith spoke. Actually, she cursed. "Something is definitely not right." She was silent for a moment and then said, "Okay. You called me for a reason. What was it?"

Pushing the hat back in her head, Sammy rubbed her forehead.

"Come on, Sammy. Don't shut me out now. What you need?"

"In all honesty, I'm not even sure. What's happened with you has thrown me all off."

"Try me. Just give me some idea on what were you thinking."

Sammy tried to piece together her jumbled thoughts. Everything seemed to be going sideways, upside down, and in every direction you could express. "Okay. One of the things I've been wondering about is why two Dutch politicians called Tuur Peeters. I mean, the whole concern about the Tour de France and other stuff just seems like b.s. to me. You know what I mean?"

"Yeah. But that's what politicians do, right? I mean, getting involved in things they shouldn't and the b.s.–"

"Under normal circumstances, I'd agree. But... I guess none of this makes any real sense. I guess...you're in Europe and you helped with the helicopter and....I don't know. The Novichok poisoning...the call....the GIGN...their disappearance! It's all so confusing, I just wanted to give Dragon a few threads to pull on. I'm not really sure what his intentions are right now but–"

"Let me go to work. We've got a number of possibilities to supply some threads. I'll call you back."

As soon as the call ended, Sammy walked over to the laptop, picked it up and returned to the dumpster. She just didn't drop the laptop inside, she threw it hard out of frustration. She was going to do the same with the cell phone - even considered setting a dumpster fire - then realized she couldn't until she'd sent the number for a new burner phone to Faith. She cursed under her breath. Nothing, nothing, nothing was going right. She turned in a tight, frustrated circle, pulled off her police hat and threw it hard against the side of the dumpster–

The police hat landed on the pavement, bounced and came to rest. Something else - thin and black - came to rest beside it.

Sammy stared at the object for a moment, puzzled. She squatted, reached to pick it up - the cop in her kicked in and she pulled her hand back. Standing up again, Sammy had a bad feeling about what she was seeing. Turning her attention to the parking lot and the coffee shop, she looked to see if someone was watching. Everything looked normal. A car was heading for the exit. A few people were talking as they crossed the parking lot, headed in for a coffee. Birds twittered in the trees behind her. Nothing seemed out of place. Except for whatever was sitting on the pavement next to her hat.

Jogging across the pavement to her car, Sammy put the cell phone in the glove box, then went back and opened the trunk, digging into the crime scene investigation kit she had put together over the years. Putting on lightweight, white cotton gloves that preventing crime scene contamination and latent prints, she jogged back across the pavement. Squatting again, Sammy lay an evidence bag next to the hat and the item. Taking apart her multifunction pen utility tool, she used the tweezers to pick up the item to examine it. It was half the size of a playing card and flexible. Holding it close to her eyes, she detected a series of circles and lines - a pattern really - on both sides. It looked like...a micro printed circuit board? Slipping it inside the evidence bag, she grabbed the hat and looked it over, trying to figure out where - the hat band inside! Someone had placed the thing inside the hat band. It was thin and flexible enough that she would never know it was in there when she wore the hat.

Jogging back across the parking lot, Sammy got into her car, put everything on the passenger seat and then popped the glove box, pulling out the burner phone. Dialing the last number that had called her, she waited with fear as the phone on the other end rang, "C'mon, c'mon–"

Someone answered but was silent.

"Faith? It's Sammy."

Sounding relieved, Faith said, "I was wondering–?"

"Have you done anything yet?"

Now Faith sounded amused, "It's only been a few minutes, Sammy. Hold your horses and I'll get–"

"*Don't* do anything until you hear from me again. Understand. *Nothing.*"

"What's wrong?"

"I'm not sure. Just trust me on this. *Don't* do anything." Sammy hung up before they could argue. She looked over at the item in the evidence bag and her jaw clenched.

Chapter 32

SAMMY KNOCKED ON the apartment door. The soft strains of a Strauss waltz sounded behind the door. But no one answered. She knocked again. He *had* to be home. She had no other plan.

Joe Oles opened the door in his face lit up in delight. Then it fell and confusion replaced it.

Holding a finger to her lips to silence him, Sammy held up a piece of paper in front of his eyes.

Joe squinted as he dug into his shirt pocket for his glasses. Slipping them on, his head moved forward reading the paper; Need help with investigation. Please don't talk. Need help with identifying an item.

When his mouth opened to say something, Sammy quickly shook her head and emphasized the finger to her lips.

Blinking several times, Joe finally stepped back, took the glasses off and motioned for her to come inside.

Sammy picked up picked up a small shopping back and went inside. Jozsef 'Joe' Oles was a Computer Engineer - a discipline that integrates several fields of computer science and electronics engineering required to develop computer hardware and software - a retired professor from a local university, and a consultant for the various police forces and intelligence agencies around the capital city. There was so much hacking, cracking, and computer crime these days, that Joe's services were in constant demand., including a couple of occasions by Evelyn O'Toole and Sammy had worked with him. As soon as Joe close the door behind her, Sammy flipped the paper over and held it out to him again.

Taking the paper in hand, Joe slipped the glasses back on and read: Case involves disappearance of Evelyn O'Toole. Please don't talk. Need to identify what this is.

As he looked at her, surprise and concern written across his face, Sammy held out the shopping bag.

Joe narrowed his eyes at her for a moment, then took the shopping bag from her and looked inside to see the clear evidence bag containing a black card. There was also the set of white gloves. Nodding in understanding, Joe gestured for her to follow him.

Sammy knew Oles lived alone, but she still listened for the presence of someone else as she followed him. The strains of another piece of music started up. The scent of Cabernet Sauvignon and aged Gouda hung in the air and Sammy noted a single glass - still half full - and a single plate of cheese and crackers sitting on a table next to an easy chair. He led her into a room she had visited once before - a bedroom he had turned into a workshop for his consulting work - and it was why she was here. There were a couple of computer workstations that she knew were loaded with a variety of specialized software, a variety of benches that held testing tools and pieces of equipment that Oles used in his work, and a workbench with a high-tech soldering station. The solder fumes had given her a headache the time she was here but she didn't detect that this time and she was grateful for a small victory. As Oles sat on a stool at one of the benches, Sammy went to one of the computer workstations and grabbed a pencil and a writing pad. Oles had the white gloves on and was examining the black item through the forensic bag.

Sammy watched him carefully remove the item and look at it closely. His brow furrowed and he adjusted his glasses. Looking closely again, flipping the item over, Oles then went to another bench and placed the black card under a powerful microscope. The thick silence that Sammy felt was only punctuated by the sound of his clothing as he flipped the item over and adjusted the microscope. He did it several times and the wait seemed endless.

Finally sitting back, removing his glasses and rubbing his eyes, Oles remained silent as he considered what he was looking at. Slipping the glasses back on after a moment, he took the black item in hand, got off the stool and walked across to another bench. As he came back toward Sammy, he had another bag in hand with the black card inside it, "It's okay. We can talk now—"

Tapping her finger against her lips frantically, Sammy shook her head no.

Oles smiled and held out the bag, "It's fine, Constable. This is a Faraday bag. It's designed for things like law enforcement digital forensics. We put a cell phone or a GPS unit inside the bag to block the signals, including satellite, Wifi, or Bluetooth frequencies and the like."

Sammy took the Faraday bag from him, looking at it with skepticism, "You're sure?"

"Yes. Now, what is about Mz. O'Toole and where did this come from?"

"It was inside my police hat. Hidden inside the sweatband. "Do you know what it is?"

Oles nodded and then gave a slight shrug, "Well, I think I know what it is." He gestured to the Faraday bag, "Those etched circles are tiny scoops to soak up sound—"

"It's a listening device?"

"That *is* what it appears to be."

"But you're not sure?"

Oles took in a short breath and let it out, "Let's just say I'm *pretty* sure. But...this is real spook stuff."

"Spook stuff?"

"Like something out of a spy novel," Oles said. "It's state of the art as far as the circuit board around the scoops is concerned. I'm not sure how it's powered, but it's pretty advanced and–"

Sammy cursed, "That's how they knew."

"That's how who knew? What's going on, Constable?"

Shaking her head, "It's better if you don't know."

"You said something about Mz. O'Toole being missing. I liked her and I'd like to help. I am cleared for–"

"I understand that." Sammy walked across the floor and grabbed the shopping bag, slipping everything inside, "But have already had someone tried to kill me over this?"

"Kill you?"

"Yes. And the person I'm working with. I don't even another person put in danger. I hope you can understand."

"Yes, of course."

Sammy headed for the door and then turned around, "Do you have any idea what the range on this thing would be?"

Oles pursed his lips, "I'm not sure. I mean... like I said, that thing is state-of-the-art but...I can't imagine it would be powerful enough to go more than a mile. But even if it's far less than that, someone could sit in a car with a parabolic microphone tuned to that thing and they could pick up every word you're saying."

"Tell me about it."

Putting and hand to his chin and stroking it, Oles said, "Of course, if the signal is going to a low-orbit, stationary satellite–"

"I get it. However they're doing it, it's working, I don't want you to say anything about this to anyone, Joe. This is highly confidential...." She looked at the man and decided he deserved more, "Evelyn O'Toole and one other person were nearly killed and I'm trying to find them."

Oles' head went back in surprise and hurt at the news.

Sammy's words were hard and bitter, "And someone is trying to prevent that. I know they're alive but someone is keeping me from finding out where they are. The thing is ... I have no idea who *they* are. That's why I need your silence."

Nodding woodenly, Oles said, "Of course. I won't say anything to anyone. If you need any more help...."

"If I need more help, I'll be back." With that said, Sammy left and She hustled downstairs to her car. A plan was forming - one that was confrontational and dangerous - but she had to do something to help Merlin Dragon. Once inside her vehicle, she set the shopping bag and its contents on the passenger seat. Then she sat back for a moment, closed her eyes and composing her words. When she was ready, she slipped on the white gloves and removed the listening device from the Faraday bag. Her heart was pounding as she spoke, and she wondered if the small scoops would pick it up and give her away, "Mr. Dragon? It's Sammy." She paused. "Yeah, I got the message from your partner." Another pause. "There's a small dock on the river at the Canadian Museum of History. We're meeting there." Pause. "Yeah, I'll do that. I have to go. I don't have much time."

Setting the listening device on the console, she started the car. Would *they* take the bait?

Chapter 33

SAMMY STOOD AGAINST the railing on the second level of the museum. Behind her was a massive wall of windows that offered the River View Salon on the other side of the glass a panoramic view of the Ottawa River and Parliament Hill on the other side. She had planned to use the Panorama Café below to watch - but this space - normally rented for events and weddings - had turned out to be empty and Sammy had used her credentials to commandeer a better view of the lawn below and the small dock at the river. It was about time something turned in her favor.

Groups of people wandered over the paths and grass areas below, snapping pictures here and there. A few more walked or stood along the river path as well some of them near the small dock area.

Sammy put a hand over her eyes again and squinted, trying to see if she could identify anyone. So far no one stood out or even seemed familiar and she began to wonder if her plan was a bust.

A large group of children - two adults in the lead - wandered across the grass on the right side and their delighted chattering and laughing carried across the air. She watched them and smiled - and then her smile dropped.

A solitary individual stood close to the building just beyond the children. He wore a plain white shirt and casual blue pants. A compact set of binoculars hung around his neck. Glancing in the direction of the children for a moment, he then raised the binoculars to his eyes and scanned the area around the dock.

Sammy watched the man lower the binoculars. Who was he?

The man glanced at the kids again, then stared at the adults for a moment. Then he looked across the grass to the Panorama Café. Lifting his head, he scanned the upper levels of the museum.

Stepping back from the railing, a sense of denial - and then betrayal swept over Sammy. And then her jaw clenched and anger burned deep in her gut. The man was Constable Devan Larkin of the West Vancouver police force.

Larkin turned his attention back to the dock.

Sammy watched him. She tried to rationalize everything. She tried to make sense of what she was seeing. He was just out for a day at the museum like everyone else - *dammit, Sammy, you know what you know. Lives are at stake. This is what it is - standard surveillance, looking for a perp. Looking for her!* Her hand touched her holstered weapon. She had changed out her standard firearm for the one she had kept wrapped in a white rag in a lock box in her trunk with her other gear. Her first mentor - the one who had recruited a teenage female to the Bear Island Police Service to empower her - had insisted on her carrying a drop gun. You never know when you might need it he had told her. But when she came to Ottawa to work for Interpol, she had stowed it in the lock box, feeling it really wasn't right to carry it. She was an honest cop and would never to justify a shooting or set someone up. But she had to admit desperate circumstances called for desperate measures. Turning on her heels, Sammy moved through the fancy dining area to the stairs and hustled through the café to the back patio. Standing in the open now, she turned her head just enough to watch him - she cursed under her breath. The group of kids was in the way. How was he going to see her-?

Several of the kids scattered, running and laughing as one of the adults tried around them up.

Sammy saw Larkin's posture stiffen. He had spotted her on the patio. Her heartbeat raced as she watched him from the corner of her eye. His body language didn't show delight at seeing her. Not like she saw back at work. Anger raced through her body when she recognized a cop spotting a perp. A number of people were walking across the grass, obviously headed towards the café patio. Sammy raised a hand - she tried to make it look discreet and yet Larkin had to see it - and she gestured with a thumb over her shoulder.

Larkin took a step, his head craning to see who she had signaled. He raised the binoculars, scanning the group of people.

That clinched it for Sammy. Her heart had told her she was wrong. Her brain now told that she was right. Larkin was looking for Merlin's *partner*. Turning around, she headed into the café, fully expecting him to follow. Striding across the café, she could see Larkin do just that - slowly at first - waiting for the entire group of people to enter the café - and then he came faster across the grass.

Once he put a foot on the patio, Larkin tried to look casual as he moved across to the doorway. Putting a hand on the handle, he looked inside.

Sammy was already at the exit to the museum, holding the glass door open - as if she had already let somebody through - she slipped through herself, letting the door slowly close behind her. Glancing over her shoulder, she saw Larkin hustled across the café. Putting her head down, she walked briskly along the curved hallway, passing through the First Peoples Of The Northwest Coast exhibit, ignoring Tsimshian Prehistory, and took the stairs to the next level. The atmosphere around her was hushed and quiet - with the exception of a few running footsteps as kids headed for something that caught their eye - but her insides were a rush of adrenaline and heartbeat.

Larkin followed at a distance.

Reaching the fourth level, Sammy glanced back discreetly. She could see the confusion written on Larkin's face as he slowly

approached the stairs at the bottom. Hustling across the floor of gallery
three for the Modern Canada exhibit, she headed for the cloth covered
entrance to gallery one. There were only one or two people that she
could see. She had been here two weeks ago with a friend and gallery
One had been undergoing renovations. Newspaper reports said the
work had been halted as a budget had been worked to for the
remainder of the new exhibits. Waiting at the edge of the drop cloth
that hung from the ceiling far above - used to prevent construction
dust and debris from getting into the other galleries - She watched
for Larkin. As soon as he appeared - and she knew he saw her - she
slipped through to the other side, into the construction area. The smell
of paint, fresh plaster and sawdust hung in the air. Hustling for the
stairs to the mezzanine that overlooked the intended gallery area below,
Sammy slipped a hand into her pocket and pulled out the white gloves.
She slipped them on and took the stairs two at a time. At the top of the
stairs, she walked twenty feet and ducked behind a pillar that stood ten
feet from the railing that overlooked the gallery below. She pulled the
drop gun and held it up near her shoulder.

Faint footsteps sounded below.

Sammy let out a cough. It echoed lightly.

There were faint footsteps that came up the stairs - paused at the
top - then moved ahead.

Taking a deep breath in and then letting it out slowly, Sammy did
her best to calm her heart rate. Counting to ten, she then stepped
around the pillar, back to the railing, and lifted her weapon with both
hands, "Freeze."

Constable Devan Larkin stopped in place. He was in the slight
crouch of a stalker, one foot ahead of the other, the compact binoculars
hanging straight down, his own weapon held low in two hands. He
slowly turned his head. And then feigned surprise, "Sammy?"

Sammy glanced over the railing. She had no idea if he was with someone. When she looked back, Larkin had pulled his foot back and was starting to turn. "I said *don't* move! I will shoot," she warned him.

His brow furrowed as Larkin looked at her, "Sammy, it's me, Devan. I don't–?"

"Weapon on the floor. *Now*," she demanded.

A sureness - maybe even a smugness - swept over Larkin's face, "You're not going to shoot me. How would it look–?"

Sammy wiggled one hand at him, "Hello? White gloves. Drop gun. Or are you too *stupid* to understand what that means?"

Larkin blinked and his brow furrowed again.

"Now place the gun on the floor."

Lifting one hand from the gun and holding it up, Larkin slowly bent over, "Okay, okay." Laying the weapon on the floor, he stood up and turned slowly to face Sammy, "I think there's been a misunderstanding–"

"You've been listening in on every conversation I've been having. I want to know why. Who put you up to it?"

Larkin shook his head, "I'm sorry, Sammy. I don't know what you're talking about–"

"I found the listening device you put in my hat."

There was a flicker behind the eyes but Larkin scrunched his nose and forehead in confusion, "A what? You're not making any sense, Sammy. If you put the gun down, we can talk about this–"

"*Stop* using my name like we're friends. It won't work." She kept the weapon trained as she wiggled a hand at him again, "You couldn't use white gloves when you handled my hat, could you? Not in the middle of the office. Latent prints are the bitch that came back to bite you." She was gambling. How could he know she hadn't run a fingerprint kit yet?

It worked. Larkin took in a breath and let it out, his face turning serious, almost angry now, "It's over, Sammy. We know what you're doing. No matter what you think this little stunt is going to do for you—"

"What the hell are you talking about? I'm trying to help—"

"You're a traitor to your own country. We know you've been feeding information to the Russians."

It was Sammy's turn to be confused. *The Russians again?* She shook her head, "Where did you get that garbage—?"

"This goes to the highest levels," Larkin shot back. "It came through the Dutch Minister of Defense, and Interpol's Secretary-General talked to me *directly* about it. He authorized me to build a case against you. It's over, Sammy."

"You're being played," Sammy told him. "This doesn't have anything to do with—"

A cold smile crossed Larkin's lips, "And you're not going to shoot me, *Constable* Powless. It's not in you to shoot an unarmed man." He rushed her.

And Sammy knew in an instant he was right. It wasn't in her. Her instincts kicked in instead. Leaving her gun hand extended as a target for him, she turned her body slightly and took a half step, bringing her left hand around to shove him against the railing, intending to pin him there and bring the gun up against the back of his head—

Larkin's lower body hit the railing and he went over, pinwheeling in the air as he tried to grab for something. A cry of terror ended with a thud that echoed in the room under construction. Larkin lay at angles a body wasn't designed for.

Chapter 34

HER HANDS SHOOK and her heart pounded in her chest as Sammy made her way through the museum, down the stairs, and out the front entrance. She had wanted to run but forced herself to maintain composure and not stand out. Her training fought against her instincts. She had thought about calling it in - he was a fellow officer - but she had an idea how it would go. Unless she could clear the bogus claims Larkin had given to justify his surveillance of her - she would be taken into custody and probably charged with his death. It still could happen if they found a way to put them together in that gallery. But there was too much at stake to simply act like an honest cop right now. There were others around her who were not acting honestly or honorably right now. And she had to play the game their way to get the job done.

Once she was back in her car, she set her hat on the passenger seat, set her elbows on the steering wheel and held her head in her hands. After she gave herself a brief respite of self-pity, Sammy grabbed her phone, checked the last text message sent to her and went to work. Her fingers were still shaky and she stabbed several times at the buttons to get the phone number in. The phone on the other end rang several times. *Come on. Come on. Come on.*

Merlin Dragon answered, his voice sleepy, "Yeah?"

"It's Sammy."

"Yeah, I could tell that."

"I'm sorry to wake you up."

"Yeah, me too. Now that we've got that cleared up, what's up?"

Sammy looked out at the tourists walking on the street. They looked so happy and carefree and she wished she could feel that way right now. "I found some kind of spy device in my hat. That's how they knew what we were doing. What we were talking about."

Merlin sounded more alert, "Who did it? Any idea?"

"Yeah. The device itself was placed by one of the constables in my office." She took in a deep breath and let it out slowly, "I set up a situation to find out who it was and it ended up in a confrontation. I had the drop on him but he still became aggressive and...it didn't go so well for him." She added quickly, "It was accidental but...."

Merlin could tell she was afraid he would think she had done something wrong, "It's okay, I understand. The question is, are you okay?"

"Just shaken up is all," Sammy said. "I don't think anybody is going to be able to place me with him at the time of his death but I'll deal with that if and when it happens. The more important thing is...he was fed a line of bull that I was passing some kind of information to the Russians. That tells me the Russian angle is bogus."

Silent for a moment, Merlin then said, "I agree. Some kind of sleight-of-hand, trying to send us in the wrong direction. The question is why?"

"I have no idea," Sammy told him. "But what I do know... is that the order to spy on me came from our good friend, the Secretary-General of Interpol."

Merlin cursed, "That guy again. I should have known."

"The thing is... I get the impression Tuur Peeters is being misled as well. I could be wrong but...."

"Why would you say that?"

"Because Larkin - that's the Constable that was spying on me - he said the Russian information came from the Dutch Minister of

Defense. I have no idea who that is. But maybe he's one of the ones who was pressuring Peeters in the first place–"

"I'll figure it out. I was thinking of going directly at the Secretary-General himself - he was the only thread we had at the time - but I'll figure out who this Dutch minister is." Merlin paused for a second, "Maybe you should stay under the radar for a while–"

"It's not going to happen. You still need someone to back you up while you're in the field. And besides - if I disappear into the woodwork - once they find Larkin's body - I'll only put the spotlight on myself. I'm sure Peeters will do enough of that when he begins to wonder why he's not getting any reports from his spy. Which is another reason I have to get to work and dig up something else we can use. I won't have much time before he finds someone else to do his dirty work and I will have to pull back."

"Okay, I appreciate it. Let's keep using the burner phones, just in case. I'll text you my next number."

The call ended and Sammy sat there for a few seconds, gathering her thoughts. There was no doubt the Secretary-General of Interpol would put the focus squarely on her once Larkin was found. She figured she had maybe twenty-four hours.

Chapter 35

TIME WAS OF THE ESSENCE. That was the phrase that kept running through Merlin's mind as he stumbled to the bathroom. Running the tap for a moment to get the water cold, he bent over and splashed it over his face. His sleep had been longer than he expected but it had also been filled with tossing and turning and dreams that he couldn't quite remember. He just knew they weren't happy dreams. His groggy mind went over the details of what Powless had told him as he headed for his cell phone - he turned right around and headed back to the bathroom - chastising himself that he had left the cold water running. He turned the tap to off and leaned with his hands against the sink. Forgetting to turn the water off was one thing - making a simple mistake like that out in the field could be deadly.

Heading back to the bed, Merlin picked up his burner phone, realizing very quickly that it was limited in its search capabilities. Reassembling and using his own special cell phone crossed his mind. But it was connected to Interpol's I-24/7 secure global police network and he still had no idea if they knew about it or were monitoring it. He picked up the telephone on the small night table and hit the button for the front desk

"Bonjour. La réception–"

"You speak English?"

"Yes of course, monsieur, how may I help you?"

"I have a strange request...."

"I specialize in strange, monsieur." There was a giggle.

Merlin couldn't help a sleepy smile, "Can you do an Internet search for me? I need to know who... I need to know the name of the person who is the Dutch Minister of Defense. I know it sounds strange—"

"One moment, monsieur."

Light music sounded as he was put on hold. It only took a few moments before the young lady came back on the line.

"I have a name for you, monsieur. Do you have something to mark down the name?"

There were a hotel notepad and a pen next to the telephone and he grabbed them, "Go ahead."

"The name is Larz Pauel Vermeeg." She spelled out the names. "He is listed as the Minister of Defense I hope that is what you are looking for?"

Merlin wrote the name and title down, "Yeah, that should be the one. Perfect."

"There is no address or location listed for this Larz Pauel Vermeeg but the information does state that the central staff for the ministry itself is located in The Hague."

"Thank you. I've got what I need."

"Is there anything else I can help you with monsieur?"

"No, nothing else. Thank you again." Merlin hung up the phone, retrieved the backpack from the small open closet near the door and set it on the bed. He slipped the cell phone he and Sammy had just used into a pocket to dispose of later in a public waste bin. Then pulled out two more burner phones. He used one of them to send a text message with the number to Sammy. He put that in his right pocket. The next one he used to punch in a number from memory with his thumbs.

The voice that answered was wary, "Yes?"

"It's Merlin Dragon."

Captain Charity Sherrell sounded relieved, "I was wondering who it was. I didn't recognize the number."

"I've had to resort to using disposable burner phones," Merlin told her. "I'm just outside of Paris." He scratched his head, "I'm not even sure where I am. I'm about an hour north - I think. Anyway, I need you to pick me up. But not in Paris. Anything close by where you can land?"

Sherrell sounded amused, "Yeah, right. You have no idea where you are and I'm supposed to land near you. Hold on."

Merlin rubbed his head as he waited, recognizing the absurdity of the situation.

"Okay. There's an airport we can use that's about an hour-and-a-half driving northeast of Paris. It's an international airport - the Beauvais-Tillé - near the city of Beauvais."

"Beauvais-Tillé Airport. I'll find it. We'll be heading to the Hague on the double."

Chapter 36

THE HAGUE, NETHERLANDS

THE BOMBARDIER GLOBAL 8000 business jet banked gently for the descent onto the runway of Rotterdam The Hague Airport. Merlin had taken a shower and was dressed in an off-the-rack a blue suit he had picked up on the way to the airport. It was a half size too big but there had obviously been no time for tailoring and he had simply cinched his special belt tighter. He had also picked up two items from an electronics store - a pack of eight-inch zip ties, used to bundle cables, and a slim digital recorder.

Captain Saab's voice came over the intercom, "Landing in five. Please buckle up. We have secured a vehicle for you - the only one left actually - at the..." She paused as if looking at a note, "At the Green Motion Car Rental counter." The intercom clicked off and then on again to add, "Good luck. We'll be on standby."

Merlin knew he would need luck, good fortune, and any other measurement that rolled the dice in his favor.

The hydraulics whined and a moment later the faint bumping sound of the landing gear landing gear locking into place sounded through the cabin.

Patting his pockets again - for the 10th or 12th time - Merlin assured himself he had the American passport, the NY Times press pass, the driver's license of Dean Mark Bell, and the zip ties and recorder in the inside pockets. The Beretta was still in the conceal holster over his right hip. The American Liberty nickel was in a back pocket. He tried to calm himself but there was always that nagging little feeling in the back of his mind that he was running out of time. Once someone found the Constable's body back in Ottawa - he pushed it from his thoughts. No sense worrying about what might happen.

The wheels barely bumped as they landed. And they had barely taxied into position when Merlin was up out of his seat, grabbed the backpack, was down the stairs and striding across the terminal to get the only vehicle they said they had left. It turned out to be a compact Mercedes Benz Smart ED, an electric drive vehicle and he was on his way driving almost silently after paying cash for three days using the Bell passport. With time rapidly running out, and now fearing he would run out of juice in this stupid car and having a hard time finding a charging station, he concluded he had to take more chances than normal. Once he was outside the airport, he pulled over and put his special cell phone together. Giving himself three minutes, he turned it on and did a quick search through the Interpol databases. In less than two minutes he found the private number and home address for Tuur Peeters and this Larz Vermeeg. He still had the hotel notepad and pen and quickly wrote the information down. Next came a quick Internet search on each individual. Both men had Wikipedia articles and he scanned through them over the next minute, absorbing the information. Time was up and he took the cell phone apart again, slipping it into the backpack.

Putting one of the addresses into the GPS unit, Merlin let it lead him on a fourteen mile trip into The Hague itself, the largest Dutch city on the North Sea. It was an amazing city, filled with modern architecture alongside centuries-old buildings. But Merlin didn't have time for sightseeing. What he did have time for was sensing the irony of chasing bad guys in a city known as a 'legal city', where somber international judges in long robes presided over notorious criminal trials. He was about to start one of his own.

The sun was setting in a reddish sky as Merlin pulled to a stop in front of a ten-story condominium building in an area of the city called Park Hoog Oostduin. This is where Larz Vermeeg had a penthouse apartment. According to the quick bio he had read, Vermeeg was in his mid-thirties and had been a fast riser in the political world. Merlin had thought about going after Tuur Peeters - actually, he relished the thought of going after the man who had created problems for the director - but Vermeeg was a better thread to pull on. It appeared he was one of the two politicians who had put pressure on Peeters. There had to be a reason why. And it was possible Peeters was only acting out of political expediency, to appease someone who might return a political favor when he needed it. A young, fast political riser usually had a power broker - maybe more than one - behind him. Someone who wanted to exert political pressure for personal reasons but didn't want to be in the spotlight. Merlin wanted to know who that was and if they had played a part in keeping them from helping O'Toole and the Director. And if so, why?

Merlin and picked up a dozen more burner phones, paid for with cash, and he used one of them now to call Vermeeg's number. If he wasn't home, he would wait–

"Hallo?"

"Mr. Vermeeg? Mr. Larz Vermeeg?"

"Ja. Wie is dit?"

"My name is Dean Bell. I'm a reporter with the New York Times in America. Do you speak English?"

There was a pause, "Yes, of course. How may I help you?"

Merlin noted the intrigue in the voice, the interest in the fact an American reporter was calling him. "My editor has sent me over to do some articles on the World Court here in your city. Since you are the head of the Ministry of Defense, and one of your mandates is protecting and enhancing the international legal system, I was hoping you may be able to–"

"Yes, yes of course. We can make an appointment to meet. I can have–"

"Actually, I was only ten or fifteen minutes away from your apartment. I was hoping we could meet, maybe just for a few minutes to start?" Merlin was playing on his obvious eagerness for some 'world class' exposure. And then he cursed himself silently. He had been too eager himself. Would Vermeeg wonder how he knew where he lived?"

There was a hesitation.

Merlin wondered if he had blown it.

Vermeeg finally said, "Yes. We can meet now. I was going to meet a young lady, but she can wait. I can call her. I am on the top floor. Buzz me when you arrive."

There was humor in the voice at standing a young lady up and Merlin was glad the man's desire for publicity and the spotlight had overridden the man's better senses. Merlin waited ten long minutes and then hustled into the entranceway of Vermeeg's building, was buzzed in and found himself in front of the politicians door within five more minutes. He turned on the digital recorder and knocked on the door. Then he stood back a few feet, a smile on his face and holding up the New York Times credentials toward the peephole.

The door swung open and a young man with curly blond hair - and a tight smile that said he was the smartest guy in the room ant room- -greeted him with an outstretched hand, "Mr. Bell, so very nice to meet you. Please come in."

Merlin shook the man's hand and stepped through the open doorway. He was sure the scent that hung across the air was marijuana.

Vermeeg closed the door behind him and strode across the living room floor toward a liquor cabinet, "Would you like something to drink before we start?"

"Anything on ice. Whiskey or–"

"I have a Belgian Owl single malt. Will that do?"

"Perfect," Merlin said.

"Please, have a seat, Mr. Bell."

As the glasses and ice clinked, and the single malt was poured, Merlin took a seat in a large easy chair across from a long white sofa and scanned the room. It was filled with antique furniture and a number of paintings on the wall - they looked old and expensive - and there was the faint sound of a television. "I hope I wasn't disturbing you. You know, with a young lady here or something?"

Vermeeg gave him a smug smile as he across the room with two drinks in his hand - one of them he passed to Merlin - "No. As I said, I was preparing to meet a young lady. No doubt, she would've ended up here later." He grinned as he sat down on this end of the sofa, crossed his legs and lifted his drink in salute, "Probably all night."

Merlin returned the gesture - and a smile - and took a sip in unison with Vermeeg. Then he placed the glass of whiskey on the coaster on the table beside him, and pulled out the hotel notebook and pen, "Perhaps we can start with a couple of questions?"

"Of course."

Shifting on the chair, Merlin raised the notebook and pen as if to start asking and writing. Instead, his lack of skill in 'social situations' kicked in and his anxiety rose. He had planned on asking some innocuous questions to start and trying to figure out who might be behind the Dutch politician. Now his mind went blank and he cursed himself.

Vermeeg's eyebrows knit together. He took another sip of his drink, watching the 'reporter' and waiting for his New York Times interview to begin.

It didn't.

Chapter 37

MERLIN DRAGON SEARCHED for a question to start with and he couldn't. His mind just wouldn't work that way. His frustration mounted. *What would Jiggs and Jaimee Hartman think of me?* And then he said to himself: *Screw it.* He looked across at the Dutchman, "Mr. Vermeeg?"

"Yes?" Vermeeg shifted slightly himself. His big break in the political world was about to begin.

"Why did you put pressure on the Secretary-General of Interpol to suppress the news of one of its directors being attacked - and nearly killed - with a Russian nerve agent?"

Vermeeg paused with his glass halfway to his lips. He blinked, "Pardon?"

"I think you heard me perfectly. What were your motives? Were they personal, political, or were they–?"

Slamming the glass down on the table beside him - the liquid splashed over the polished surface - Vermeeg rose to his feet, his face a mass of indignation, "I don't know what you are driving at but I'm going to ask you to leave. Now!"

Merlin calmly set the pencil down on his lap, leaned forward slightly, reached under the half-size too-big jacket, and pulled his Beretta. He gestured with it, "I suggest you sit down. We're not finished with the interview."

Vermeeg sputtered with indignation, "Interview? This is no interview. This is...this is...slander!"

Standing up, the notebook and pen falling to the floor, Merlin held the gun at the man's head, "I wouldn't test my patience. I'm tired and I'm irritated. Sit - down."

The look of indignation disappeared and was replaced with one of fear. Vermeeg licked his lips, swallowed, and he sat down, "I... I don't understand... I have no idea–"

"And if you lie to me, I'm only going to be *more* irritated. Do you understand me?"

Vermeeg nodded woodenly, and then shrugged a shoulder, "I'm afraid...that you have the wrong person and...."

Merlin took a step and aimed the weapon directly between his eyes, "Then I guess I'm wasting my time and I don't need you."

The Dutchman put his hands out as if to ward off the bullet, "Please, no. I beg of you. I really don't know anything–"

"You pushed Tuur Peeters to halt the investigation based on crap like the Tour de France and some art fair. Why?"

Vermeeg looked stunned, "How...how did you know that? Who are you–?"

"Someone who is really pissed at having two friends poisoned by you and your pals." Merlin bared his teeth, his anger rising to the surface, "Last chance."

"Ik was het niet. Ik was het niet. Het was niet mijn idee," Vermeeg said in desperation. He closed his eyes in anguish and banged a fist against his forehead, "Engels - English, English." He looked up at Merlin, his eyes pleading, "I mean, it was me but... it wasn't my idea."

"Whose idea was it?"

"Francisca Daane. It was Francisca Daane. She was the one who came to me." He pumped a fist in anger, "Verdomme! Ik vertelde haar–"

Merlin spoke sharply to get the man to focus, "Enough. Who is she?"

Vermeeg closed his eyes and took a breath to compose himself, "Yes. Francisca is the Minister of Justice and Security."

"Why? Why did she want the investigation stopped? What's her game?"

"Game? Oh. Yes." Vermeeg shrugged a shoulder, "It was something someone she knows wanted to happen." The Dutchman held a hand up, "And no, I don't know who it was." He wiped the hand over his face, "All I did was...do her a favor. She is about to become a Deputy Prime Minister and...."

"And you saw an opportunity to advance your own career."

"Something like that."

Merlin felt deep disgust at the man's willingness to hurt others in order to advance himself. He bent down, picked up the pen and notebook and tossed it to the sofa, "Write down her address and phone number."

Vermeeg picked up both and wrote in the notebook. Finished, he held both out to Merlin, "Perhaps I can make amends by setting up a meeting with her tonight?"

Taking the pen and notebook from the man, Merlin slipped them into the side pocket of the one-size-too-big jacket, "Right. And you just have to speak Dutch and screw me over."

"No, no, no. I will be speaking English," Vermeeg insisted. "You will understand everything I say."

"And why would you do this?"

Vermeeg looked at the weapon, "So you don't shoot me. You look like a man I can trust."

"Right." Merlin considered the man's offer for a moment. Then he gestured with the Beretta, "Go ahead. Make the call. But send any kind of signal and–"

"I know, I know." The Dutchman got up slowly, hands up near his shoulders, and walked across to the liquor cabinet.

"Let me see what you're doing."

Vermeeg turned his body slightly to let Merlin see, picked up a cell phone slowly turned, hands still up near his shoulders, "I will call now." He slowly brought the phone down and began swiping on the screen, then tapped, and held the phone up near his ear. It was only a few minutes that he stood there, but the time seemed to drag on and actually seemed to weigh heavy on Vermeeg, no doubt worrying that she wouldn't answer – his face brightened, "Ja. Hallo, Francisca." He grimaced and switch to English, "This is Larz. Yes. Yes. Uh...I have here a reporter from the New York Times in America. Yes, yes, America. Well, he wanted to interview me. It's all about how our city and our country are so tied up in international justice. Yes, yes. He was...uh... heading back to New York and I suggested he might want to interview you before he does. Do you have a moment tonight?" There was a pause as he listened. Then he nodded, "Yes, yes. I will give him your address and he will be there shortly. Thank you. Yes, you're very welcome." He ended the call, "You are to go there now." Vermeeg flashed a smile, "So we are good?"

Chapter 38

BENOORDENHOUT, THE Hague

PULLING TO A STOP on the circular brick driveway an hour after sundown and getting out, Merlin Dragon surveyed the red brick house. Actually, it was more like a two-story villa, with the soft lights in the windows giving it a storybook feeling. It seemed strange, coming here to meet someone who had been evil enough to participate in the attempted assassination of the Director and O'Toole. Then again, maybe ogres lived in glass houses too. Merlin had left Vermeeg zip-tied hand and foot - and then hogtied - in his bathtub. He warned the politician not to mess around too much trying to escape and accidentally turn the water on. He doubted anyone would find him before morning and hopefully everything else would be tied up by that time as well. The neighborhood was spacious, with a number of large homes, separated by green spaces and everything was calm and quiet as Merlin climbed the four steps to the front door.

The front door swung open before he even knocked and a woman in her forties appeared in the doorway. She was tall, wore a dark pantsuit, had short and curly dark blonde hair and a finely chiseled face.

The light scent of rose perfume hung in the air. She smiled and held her hand out, "Mr. Bell? I'm Francisca Daane, Please come in."

Merlin shook her hand and stepped through the doorway. As she closed the door behind him, he noted the open concept allowed a view right through the heart of the house. The furniture looked like highly polished, exquisite antiques. Wondering if they were real, he slipped a hand into a pocket and held out his press pass and credentials, "Just to verify I am who I say I am."

Daane held up a hand as she walked past him, "If Larz vouched for you, I am fine. Please come in and sit down."

Slipping the identification back into his pocket, Merlin discreetly made sure the recorder the on-button was engaged and running as he followed her, "You have a beautiful home here."

"Thank you. It was my husband's family home." Daane sat down in a large easy chair next to a fireplace and crossed her legs, "He passed away some years ago."

Merlin sat in a chair just to her right, "I'm sorry to hear that."

Daane flashed him a brief smile, "Thank you. Now, shall we get down to why you are here?"

Leaning over and pulling at the notebook and pen, Merlin said, "You're a woman of few words. You get right to the point."

"I find it better that way. Saves a lot of time and trouble. What would you like to know?"

Merlin considered trying to go through the charade of an interview this time but decided it wasn't worth the time and effort. He put the pen and notebook back in his pocket, leaned forward and pulled the Beretta, laying it across his knee, "I like your personal philosophy. It's better if we get right down to the nitty-gritty. Larz tells me you were the one behind impeding an investigation into the attempted assassination of two members of Interpol. You used your political influence - with help from Larz - to get Interpol's Secretary-General, Tuur Peeters to pressure investigators to back off."

Daane raised an eyebrow and then nodded, "Yes. That is true."

That set Merlin back, "You admit it?"

The Dutch woman shrugged, "Of course. Why would I deny it if I did it?"

Merlin narrowed his eyes and studied the woman's face, "So you admit impeding an investigation for political purposes? Because of some stupid bike race and some art convention?"

Waving a hand, Daane said, "Oh, no, no. That had nothing to do with it."

Closing his eyes for just a moment, Merlin rubbed his forehead. None of this made sense. He looked across at the woman again, "Why would you impede an investigation–?"

"Oh, it wasn't just the investigation. It was everything from the beginning."

"From the beginning...?"

Daane nodded nodded somberly as she looked across at him, "Yes. It was all done with one purpose in mind. To draw you out...Mr. Dragon."

Chapter 39

SITTING THERE DUMBFOUNDED, Merlin's mind flashed back over the conversation since she had opened the door to greet him, trying to remember if he had accidentally used his own name. He was sure he hadn't. Of course, his thoughts were divided, also warning him about the gun barrel pressed against his skull just behind his right ear.

Francisca Daane smiled as if it were a tea party, stood up in a crouch and reached across to take the Beretta from Merlin's hand, "I'll take that, thank you very much." She sat back down, the weapon now in her lap, and crossed her legs, getting comfortable again, "We wouldn't want anybody to get hurt now, would we?"

Merlin's mind continued to whirl even as he kept statue-still because of the possibility a bullet could come crashing through his brain. He asked Daane the only question that mattered right now, "How did you know?"

Daane didn't answer. She simply continued to sit there with a pleasant look on her face.

A footstep sounded to Merlin's right and he swiveled his eyes in that direction. A husky man in a blue suit appeared. The bearing was military. Instinctively moving his head to look up at the man's face, the gun barrel was pressed hard against his skull and he winced. Blue-suit held out something next to his face.

Merlin saw Daane look to blue-suit, at whatever he was holding, and then at him.

There was silence for a moment and then Daane asked, "Is it him?"

Blue-suit's voice was deep, with a heavy Dutch accent, "Yes." He switched from English to Dutch, "We zullen het vanaf hier nemen."

Daane seemed to both pleased and relieved, "Goed. Groeten aan meneer VanDaele. Ik zal zijn volledige steun verwachten."

Merlin had no idea what she had said but something in the foreign words tickled his brain. He didn't know what it was but he closed his eyes for a moment, trying to burn the sounds of the words into his memory. It wasn't easy with a foreign language but something told him it was important–

"Stand up," blue-suit ordered.

The gun barrel nudged his skull.

Merlin did as he was told, moving slowly.

Blue suit put a hand on his elbow and pushed on it, "Turn. Put your hands behind your back."

Again doing as he was told, Merlin glanced over at Daane. The pleased look now took on a tinge of smugness. He felt and heard zip ties binding his wrists together as other hands patted him down. The men were efficient, well trained. They found the false credentials, the small recorder, the keys to the Mercedes as well as the half-dozen zip ties of his own.

Daane smiled as she looked at the zip ties pulled from his pocket, "Why, Mr. Dragon, were you planning on some type of bondage relationship with me?" Her laughter was light but mocking.

A moment later, Merlin's view of Daane disappeared when a bag was jammed over his head. The sound of the light, mocking laughter remained. He was pulled away from the chair, turned to his left, and then a second hand clamped on his other elbow and he was marched across the room. He heard a door open moments later and felt the coolness of the night air wash over his skin as he was taken outside. He stumbled down the steps, only kept upright by the strong hands holding his elbows. He heard a door slide open. It sounded like on the side of a van – he suddenly felt himself propelled by a hand on his back and he landed face down on a cold steel floor. Hands grabbed his ankles and they were zip tied together as well. A moment later, he was hogtied and there was the sound of the door sliding closed behind him. Merlin found it ironic that he had left Vermeeg in a bathtub in the very same condition.

The two doors on the van opened and closed and the engine was started.

Merlin felt himself rock as the van accelerated. He considered his next move. Should he wait and see where they were taking him? He wanted to find out who they were working for but his instincts told him he would never get that opportunity. More than likely they would shoot him or cut his throat and simply dump his body somewhere. It would be ten minutes or so before they would be in an area with more traffic and the houses closer together - he corrected himself - it was possible they were headed farther out of town and he might not be able to find his way back to his rental car very easily. He had to keep in mind that time was running out for both him and Sammy Powless. He forced himself over on his side to keep from rocking and went to work. Being hogtied was actually a bit of an advantage. With his hands forced behind his back, they were closer to his back pocket. But he still had to put a strain on his muscles and his arms began to shake as he felt with his fingers for the back pocket where he had the American Liberty nickel. Finally securing it in his fingers, he moved slowly, remembering how he had dropped the key when the gendarmes had first arrested him and cuffed him at the hospital. He couldn't afford that here. Feeling the surface of the coin with his thumb, he found the head-side, flipped it over at to face upward, slid a fingernail clockwise along the edge and voilà - the small blade of hardened stainless steel rotated out. Carefully searching for the zip tie that connected his hands to his feet, he found it and cut it. His muscles immediately felt the relief but he had no time to relax. In fact, he was going to have to move fast from this point because of the noise he was about to create.

It was going to be difficult if not impossible to arch his back and bring his feet up behind him to cut the ties around his ankles. And there was no way he could maneuver the coin's blade to cut the ties binding his wrists. He had to use a simple force technique instead. Lifting his bound hands away from his body, he brought them back sharply and hit them as hard as he could against his butt. The zip ties broke open with a sharp snap that echoed off the walls of the van.

"Wat was dat lawaai?"

"Ik weet het niet. Controleer de gevangene!"

Merlin moved quickly, rolling over and pulling the bag off his head - he panicked - he had lost the coin. In the passenger seat, a large man with a blond buzz cut was turning to look at him.

When buzz cut saw the prisoner's hands were free in front of him, he swore, unbuckled and began to climb between the seats.

Turning on his butt, Merlin pulled his zip tied feet back and slammed them hard into the man's face.

Buzz cut grunted and slumped for a moment. But it was only a moment and his eyes met Merlin's, his face now a mask of rage.

Merlin heard the driver unbuckle as well and knew he didn't have much time - it would soon be two to one - his hands swept out, seeking the coin. He winced when his finger was nicked by the hardened blade. Bringing his feet back again, he slammed them once more into buzz cut's head as his fingers picked up the coin.

The big blond man barely felt the blow this time. His rage was building.

Bringing his hand around, Merlin slashed across the man's throat with the small blade.

Buzz cuts eyes went wild as he grabbed for his throat. Blood began spurting between his fingers.

Merlin rolled away from the big man. As soon as buzz cut fell face down on the van's floor, Merlin cut through the zip ties around his ankles, was up in a crouch and stepped on the big man's back–

The man in the blue suit was bringing a Glock 17M handgun around with one hand while trying to drive with the other.

Striking quickly, Merlin brought the blade down hard on the man's wrist.

A gunshot echoed painfully off the van walls.

The driver cried out in pain - the blade was embedded in sinew and bone - and he dropped the handgun.

He also lost control of the van.

It skidded sideways, the tires squealing in agony. And then it flipped.

Merlin reached for something - anything - but he caught air and a moment later his back slammed into something solid.

The van flipped again and slid off the road, the roof buckling as it slammed into a centuries-old European beech tree.

Chapter 40

MERLIN CLIMBED FROM THE FOG, trying to make sense of where he was. His legs were higher than his head for some reason. He tried to lower them but his body protested in a hard spasm and he squeezed his eyes shut. He opened them slowly again - then the memory of the van flipping came flooding back and instincts told to get his hands up, ready to fight. But his body protested again and he struggled to keep them in a defensive posture. He moved his head slowly to lessen the spasms and realized he was actually lying on the inner wall of the van, his right shoulder pressed up against a seat - was that the passenger seat? To his left lay the body of the man he had cut across the throat. Blood was still pouring out but the van was tilted slightly and the blood pool was forming towards the back doors. Using the edge of the seat with his right hand, Merlin slowly pulled himself into a sitting position, looking for the other man. The Glock 17M was sitting not far from his feet and he rolled to his knees, quickly grabbing it and fighting off the nausea from an intensely sore back. He figured he must've slammed his back onto the floor of the van - hell, it could have been the ceiling or the side, the way they were rolling. He caught sight of a brown buzz cut over the edge of the seat and he brought the handgun up.

But there was no movement. The man in the blue suit lay with his back against the passenger door, his head lying at an awkward angle. He had been unbuckled, turned at an angle and in pain - all detrimental to instinctively protecting yourself in a rollover.

Merlin knew he had to move quickly. He glanced through the front windshield - it was actually gone and he could feel the night air. It was dark and a few lights were going on in the houses. It wouldn't be long before people came out to see the accident. Stepping through the gap between the two seats, Merlin searched blue suit and found the fake credentials, the keys to the Mercedes, a folded piece of thick paper and his recorder. The blade of the American Liberty nickel was still stuck in his bloody wrist and Merlin pulled it free, wiping the blood on the man's suit Stepping through the windshield opening, he closed the blade and slipped the coin into his back pocket. The sharp, up and down wail of a Dutch police siren sounded in the distance. Checking for the skid marks - the start of them gave his direction back to Francisca Daane's house - he set off, slipping the weapon into his conceal holster as he limped and hobbled.

Ten minutes into his limping hike back to the house, he paused to rest his sore back. Curious as to the thick piece of folded paper Mr. Blue Suit had in his pocket, Merlin slipped it out and unfolded it. His initial surprise was forcefully replaced by anger. Anger at himself for a past mistake that had come back to bite the Director and O'Toole. Slipping it back into his pocket, he began limping his way again, infused with more anger and determination to get to the bottom of this.

It took some time before he finally spotted his rental car sitting off the road in the circular driveway. The long walk had given him time to think - and for his anger to build. The two men who had taken them prisoner had appeared to be military - or maybe ex-military working for somebody. The military bearing. The training. The Glock 17M semiautomatic pistol. The folded piece of paper. It was beginning to add up. One of the Dutch words Daane used in her conversation with the two men rattle around in his brain. It was familiar. Now he had to find out if his feelings were right.

The downstairs lights in the house were off. There were two lights on upstairs. Climbing the steps to the front door, Merlin scanned the houses on either side as he dug into the webbing of a special belt. The houses were far enough away and the trees made it difficult for anyone to see him very well. The street was quiet, and the host on the other side of the street was dark. Turning back to the door, Merlin knelt and went to work with his lock picks. It took him less than twenty seconds. Practice made perfect. Slipping the tools back into the webbing, Merlin pulled the Glock 17 and entered the house, closing the door quietly behind him.

It only took him a few minutes to find the stairs and he climbed to the second floor. Light spilled from an open doorway halfway down the hallway and he crouched low, moving in that direction. Pressing himself against the wall, Merlin peered around into the room. It was a softly lit bedroom containing a king-size bed and light-colored furniture. The low sound of a television was off to the left.

Francisca Daane stood sideways next to a chair that had a fluffy white robe draped over the back. She wore a pink, satin-and-lace baby doll nightgown that barely covered her. The scent of lilac bubble bath carried across the air and she was busy rubbing a cream into her face.

Turning his head and checking the dark hallway in both directions, Merlin listened for the sounds of anyone else in the house. Did she have a bodyguard or two? He hadn't seen any before but that didn't mean they weren't there. He would just have to deal with whatever happened. Slipping a hand into a pocket, Merlin turned on the digital recorder, then he stepped around the door frame into the room, keeping the weapon up and sweeping just in case.

Hearing the footsteps, Daane turned, a look of surprise in her face. It only took a moment before the self-assured look he had seen before returned. She turned to face him, now rubbing the cream into her hands. Tilting her head, she gave him a coy smile, "Why, Mr. Dragon, are you back to use the zip ties on me?" She held her hands out to the side, displaying her shapely body, "As you can see, I am quite ready to play your games. Should we move to the bed now? Or do you prefer to be the one who issues the–?"

"Put the robe on."

Daane gave him a mock pout, "Are you sure we can't trade–?"

"Do it now."

Merlin watched her emphasize the pouty behavior as she picked up the fluffy robe and slipped it on.

"Thank you, now we can talk."

Raising an eyebrow, Daane looked down at the Glock, "I highly think we can have a civilized conversation while you're holding that...weapon...on me. It could go off and it's making me nervous." She slipped her hands into the pockets on the robe and looked him in the eye, waiting.

Lowering the weapon, Merlin gave her a slight nod, "Okay, You got what you wanted. Now you start to–"

Daane pulled a handgun from the right pocket of her robe. Scowling, she aimed it at Merlin's heart and pulled the trigger.

Click.

Startled, Daane looked at the weapon in her hand, looked at Merlin and pulled the trigger again.

Click. Click. Click.

Shaking his head, Merlin stepped forward and pulled the weapon from her hand. It was his own special Beretta. Stepping back away from her, he slipped the Beretta into his conceal holster, "This is *my* gun, remember? It only works with my palm print."

The Dutch politician merely shrugged and slipped her hands back into the robe's pockets, "Well, you can't blame me. You did break into my house–"

Merlin stepped forward, sticking the gun in her face, "Oh no you don't. Hands out of your pockets. Now."

Daane put her hands up near her shoulders as Merlin patted her pockets and she gave him a smile, "Do you like the feel of my body, Mr. Dragon? Perhaps if you pat a little higher? Or lower, if you prefer–?"

"Shut up." Satisfied she had no other weapons in the pockets, Merlin stepped back, "You said this whole thing was set up to draw me out. Who's idea was it?"

Hands in her pockets, Daane lifted her shoulders up near her ears in an I-have-no-idea gesture, "I'm afraid you must have misunderstood me, Mr. Dragon. Why would I say such a thing?"

Merlin looked at her, standing there looking so innocent, without the slightest evidence of fear in her face. Simple social situations were difficult for him at the best of times, but Merlin felt completely out of his depth with this slick, lying politician. One who was willing to pull every trick in the book.

Chapter 41

THERE HAD TO BE A WAY to get her to talk. Merlin half-way considered asking her if she had an ironing board he could use to waterboard her in her tub. Presuming she had a tub. Maybe she only had a shower. And he highly doubted Daane was the kind of woman to iron her own clothes - more likely the dry cleaning type. All that useless verbiage rolled through his mind as he stood looking at a woman who was sure she had the upper hand. And in many ways she was right. He wasn't going to torture her, although the thought surfaced a couple of times. Desperate measures and desperate people and all that. A different tactic came to mind. Good cop - bad cop - lying cop.

"I would get ahead of this thing if I were you," he told her. "Your career is about to go down the tubes."

Danae's eyebrows knit together, "What are you talking about?"

"Your friend Larz Vermeeg is already spilling his guts to the authorities–"

"That's ridiculous," Daane shot back. "Larz would never–"

Merlin raised his voice, "Your friend Larz is the one who called you and sent me over here as a New York Times reporter, right? He already told me it was *your* idea to push Tuur Peeters to halt the investigation into what happened in Paris. He said it was *your* idea to use the Tour de France and all those other events as a political motive."

Daane sneered, "That little shit doesn't know a thing."

"That little shit as you call him is very ambitious. You're not the only one who's interested in moving up and he just *had* to dig to figure out what was behind your motive to recruit him." Pulling the folded piece of paper from his pocket, Merlin unfolded it and held it out for Daane to see, "I got this from your two pals who used it to identify me."

Daane stared at it. It was the mug shot and information on Merlin when he had been arrested on his second assignment in Kralendijk on Bonaire, an island in the Leeward Antilles in the Caribbean Sea. The island, along with Sint Eustatius and Saba, was a special municipality within the country of the Netherlands.

"This is just *more* evidence that people inside and connected to the Dutch government are involved in a conspiracy," Merlin told her. "Interpol is already working with the Dutch government to turn Larz Vermeeg over to the French. They don't take kindly to interference in their legal affairs and those National gendarmes guys can't wait to get their hands on him."

Daane licked her lips.

"I would suggest you get ahead of the curve. You've heard of the term prisoner's dilemma? In order for a conspiracy to succeed, every person involved has to keep his or her mouth shut or stick to the same exact story that everyone else is telling. The first person who gives it up usually has the information required to make a deal. They go free and the rest...? Well, it's like dominoes, one topples after the other. Unless another prisoner has information that the first doesn't have–"

Cursing and crossing her arms across her chest, Daane spit out the words, "That damn VanDaele said it would be easy."

Bingo. Merlin's feelings had been right. Dirk VanDaele was a global arms dealer who owned Schorpioen Internationale here in the Netherlands. The Netherlands was a top tax haven for many of the world's biggest arms dealers and VanDaele worked with them all as the middleman, taking much of the risk. His global dealings involved everything you needed to carry out a war, ranging from small arms and light weapons (and their parts, accessories, and bullets) to machine guns, mortars, rocket-propelled grenades, flamethrowers, grenade launchers, anti-tank weapons, tanks, fighter planes, and ballistic missiles. His partner was Davet Minard, another global arms dealer who owned DVM International, a Private Military Contractor registered in Gibraltar. Both men were suspected of supplying the funds to finance terrorism and create instability around the world to create work and sales for their companies. In fact, the two men had been using their own bank - Banque Monégasque de la Finance in Monte Carlo - to offer great loans to emerging nations in a plan to eventually fleece them from their wealth. It was Merlin who had ruined their plans with an African country and he was trying to take down VanDaele at his guarded compound in Bonaire when he was arrested. Merlin foolishly set off a makeshift bomb at the compound in the hopes of luring his target into a less secure hotel room while the matter was investigated and repaired. The authorities had put a call into Interpol Canada and that was the call Sammy Powless had recalled; *You're the same Dragon on Bonaire? I'm the one who took the call from the Kingdom Representative.* Merlin wondered if that call was the reason O'Toole had put him and Sammy together. Keep it in a tight circle? It didn't matter right now. More importantly, VanDaele *or* Minard had the connections to bring in someone like the woman who had attacked the Director and O'Toole. They were more powerful working together - was that what he was up against? He asked VanDaele, "Was Minard involved with it as well?"

Daane's Eyebrows pushed together hard again, "Minard?" She shook her head, "No, not that I know of. I know of him but I've never met him."

Merlin tried to read the woman. "Are you sure? Whose idea was it to hire the team of assassins?"

"Team?"

"The man and the woman."

" I...I don't know."

Merlin narrowed his eyes. Did he detect a smirk? If it was there, it was replaced by anguish in a heartbeat.

Daane's face screwed up and a few tears fell. She turned, wiping her eyes, "I'm sorry. I need a tissue." She headed for the nightstand on this side of the bed, brushing away a tear from her left cheek, "I can't believe this is happening. All I wanted to do was help my country. That's all I was trying to do."

"Hey, hold on." Merlin moved after her.

Daane waved a hand back at him as she bent over and pulled open a small drawer, "Don't worry, I'm just a silly woman–"

Merlin heard the sound of wood sliding over wood and he instinctively leaned to his right.

Whirling around, Daane brought a small handgun up and fired.

Pain ripped over Merlin's left shoulder. He brought up his weapon and fired.

Daane staggered back a step, a stunned look on her face as she put a hand to her chest. Red blood blossomed on the white robe under her fingers. Her body toppled backward, smashed into a lamp, rolled to the right and landed face down.

Merlin kept the gun on her. There was no movement. He moved forward, kicked the gun away, bent over and reached out to check the pulse on her neck–. Agonizing, burning pain shot through his left arm and he realized her bullet had grazed the outside of his shoulder. Holding the gun between his knees, he checked for a pulse.

Dead.

Chapter 42

GETTING BACK INTO THE RENTED MERCEDES, Merlin started the vehicle, kept the lights off and rolled into the street. Everything was quiet in the neighborhood and he doubted anyone heard the shots. The houses were too far apart. He had wiped his fingerprints clean in the house - he hadn't really touched anything - and he had wiped the prints from the gun, leaving it next to the body. It would likely be traced back to Mr. blue-suit, lying dead in the rolled van. He had stuffed a washcloth from her bathroom under his shirt over the bullet graze. It wasn't really bleeding, it just hurt a lot. But what hurt more was losing the politician before he could get more information from her. Something had changed in their conversation. When he had asked about the team of assassins, he had the impression she came to the realization that he didn't know as much as he was letting on. He cursed himself. He was going to have to learn to be a better interrogator. Yeah, just add that to the long list of things I need to get better at.

Merlin felt anger settle in. He wasn't sure if it was just because of what had happened to the Director and O'Toole or if he was beginning to get angry with himself. He felt like he was spinning his wheels, getting nowhere. He slapped his phone back together and checked Interpol's 24-7 network. Dirk VanDaele was all he had left if he was going to stop a team of assassins from getting to their targets. With a nagging feeling a Dutch elite SWAT team had been assembled after his last search and were only waiting for another signal to zero in on him,, he began to sift through the records to find out where the man was. Hopefully, it was at some place here and not just in the Caribbean. His clearance as The Stopper allowed him to move through cyberspace and penetrate Dutch tax records. It was the most direct way of finding property the arms dealer owned. It was also a way to trigger an alert. Hopefully, Director Laurent had enough safeguards in place that he was actually undetectable. But with Interpol's Secretary-General, Tuur Peeters seemingly being an 'inside man' and working against him, anything was possible. He found three properties. One in the Caribbean. One in South Africa. And one in some place called Gronsveld here in the Netherlands. A quick Internet search showed it was a three to four hour drive to the southeast. Gronsveld was on the outskirts of Maastricht and the Maastricht Aachen Airport just to the north could handle the Global 8000.

Pulling his special cell phone apart again, Merlin grabbed one of the burner phones and was on his way back to The Hague Airport. There was no sense sitting around and waiting for that potential SWAT team to zoom in on him. He alerted Sherrell and Saab that he was on the way - received a confirmation that the airport could handle the business jet - and began to formulate a plan to not only pull on this thread but to yank it out of the arms dealer's body.

Chapter 43

OTTAWA, CANADA

A SOFT KNOCK sounded in the distance. Sammy Powless stirred and sat up, running a hand over her face. She had fallen asleep after working for hours on her laptop. It was still running, the screensaver of colored ribbons flowing gently. The scent of stale coffee hung in the air, her half-finished coffee now sitting cold next to the laptop on the coffee table in front of her. Hands in her head now, Sammy stretched her back. She wasn't even sure what time it was, or how long she'd been working on digging up something to help Merlin Dragon.

The soft knock sounded again. It was coming from her apartment door.

Sammy looked at her wrist. And then realized she wasn't wearing her watch. She'd changed into her tracksuit and left it—

There was a soft click.

And then her door swung open, banging back against the wall.

That took Sammy by surprise, she had a deadbolt lock and—

Two men in staid-gray suits moved inside, taking up a tactical stance on either side of the doorway, handguns up and sweeping the room.

Jumping to her feet, Sammy considered rushing for her weapon in the bedroom. It was in a lock box but maybe - she discarded that thought when the guns came to bear on her.

"Don't move," one of the men yelled at Sammy.

Sammy did as told, raising her hands.

The man turned his head slightly and called back through the open doorway, "We have eyes on the target on the right. We need the rest of the apartment cleared,"

Four more men rushed low into the room, guns held in both hands until they cleared the first two men and then they fanned out to check the rest of the apartment.

Two more men entered. The man in the lead jabbed a finger at her, Constable Samantha Kamino'ckama Powless?"

He had butchered the second name and Sammy corrected him, "That's pronounced Kamin-noke-kama."

"Whatever." He held a cell phone up, looking from its screen to her.

The last man coming in and trailing the others asked, "Is it her?"

"Yeah, it's her." The man slipped the cell phone in a pocket and gestured to Sammy, "Sit down. And keep your hands where we can see them."

"I'll sit when I want to sit. Who are you and–?"

The last man continued walking, slipped something into his suit coat's pocket and then pulled out a folded piece of paper, handing it to Sammy, "I don't have to tell you squat. Read this."

Sammy took it in hand. She knew what he had slipped into his pocket. It was a LockPick gun. It was originally developed for police to allow them quick entry without having to learn lock picking methods. It explained how they were able to open her deadbolt lock. She stood woodenly as she heard 'clear' being shouted from the various rooms in her apartment. A moment later, the men clearing the apartment reappeared one by one, guns holstered and now snapping powder-free Nitrile gloves into place as they began a forensic search.

One of the men walked to the coffee table, slammed the laptop lid closed without turning the computer off and slipped it under his arm.

"Hey! What are you doing?" Sammy asked.

Mr. last-man-in gestured to the paper, "Read it like I told you. It will explain everything." He gestured to the others and barked out orders, "Take all computers, cell phones, electronic devices you find. Search everything. No stone unturned, gentlemen."

Sammy unfolded the paper and looked at it. It was a warrant issued by a judge that allowed agents of CSIS - Canada's spy agency - to do exactly what was happening, 'to enter her place, to search for, remove or return, or examine, take extracts from or make copies of or record in any other manner the information, record, document or thing; or to install, maintain or remove any thing'. The wording was specific and broad. The paperwork also showed that CSIS had supplied the judge with documents showing they had obtained the approval of the Minister of Public Safety and Emergency Preparedness to target her. Everything was wrapped up tightly in a bureaucratic ball of b.s. She felt angry and shook her head, "Okay, fine. Take everything and get out."

Mr. Last-man-in gestured for her to step forward, "You're coming with us as well."

Baring her teeth, Sammy said, "The Canadian Security Intelligence Service doesn't have the powers to arrest me. And since I don't see a member of the RCMP or the Ottawa police, you can—"

"We're not arresting you." Mr. last-man-in gave her a cheeky grin, "We are merely detaining you on the basis of protecting Canada's interests against foreign-influenced activity that is detrimental to Canada's safety and security."

Confusion reigned over Sammy's world. She had expected this but not exactly this. As CSIS agents, they didn't have to identify themselves or give her any information. With a spy agency, covert actions and secrecy are inherently understood and par for the course. Normal rules, regulations, and laws were out the window in many respects. She didn't have to answer any questions but there was no telling what they could do under a charge of being detrimental to the country itself.

Mr. Last-man-in was growing impatient with her just standing the and he gestured for her to step forward again, "Come on, sweetheart, let's go."

Sammy snarled at him, "I'm not your sweetheart."

"We have a bag of burner phones." One of the agents held up a shopping bag from the Vine Boutique in the nearby mall.

Letting out a breath of frustration before she could stop it, Sammy knew she was getting in deeper. She had used the shopping bag to hold two dozen fresh burner phones, ready to use. There was no doubt they would make her look like any one of foreign-influenced agent, spy, agent provocateur or traitor. Or all of the above.

Turning his head to look at the shopping bag, Mr. Last-man-in asked, "Any of them look like they've been used? Anything we can use?'

The agent shook his head, "No, it doesn't look like any of them been used yet."

Mr. Last-man-in called out to the other agents searching the apartment, "Anybody find another cell phone? Anybody?"

A muffled yell came from the bedroom, "Yeah. I got something here."

Sammy felt her jaw tighten as another searcher appeared, a burner phone in hand, gloved hand tapping at the screen. She had memorized Merlin's next phone number but she had sent a text message to it with the number for this phone. She'd erased the message but would they be able to find it?

Hustling over to his agent, Mr. Last-man-in looked at the screen without touching it, "Anything on it? Anything we can use?"

"Not that I can see."

"Okay. Get this phone over to out tech experts with the others. Have them look at this one first. There has to be a reason it wasn't with the others. And put a rush on it."

"Got it."

Sammy reigned herself to being put into the 'system' - actually, that wasn't true. She had no idea where she was headed. Or what kind of 'system' - maybe a black hole site somewhere where she would never be found or heard from again. Everything was now on Merlin Dragon and what he could do.

Chapter 44

GRONSVELD, NETHERLANDS

MERLIN SAT IN a rental SUV just ten minutes south of Maastricht. It was a couple of hours before sunup and he was using a pair of military night vision binoculars he had taken from the plane to get a view of the house through the trees. Actually, it was a castle. A small castle but nonetheless Margraten Castle had been turned into a home by Dirk VanDaele. And the good part about that was the fact an architectural magazine had done an extensive article on the transformation, complete with pictures of the inside that could be easily found on the Internet. There had been a lot of controversy when he had started knocking out a lot of the smaller rooms to create a more modern living area. But like a true bully, VanDaele had fought everybody, spending a small fortune on a court case to do what he wanted to do. With a basic understanding of what he would find inside the four-story stone structure, Merlin now had to find a way to get inside. Despite the thick band of trees on the outer edges of the property, there was a lot of open space a man had to cover before he reached the house itself.

A circular stone fortification stood off to the left of the house, and they were joined together by a wide stone hallway. Merlin decided approaching the hosts from that direction offered him some concealment from the upper windows of the main house. Unless, of course, guards were stationed on top of the circular fortification. In which case, he'd be picked off before he reached within one hundred yards of his target. But what choice did he have–? Merlin nearly jumped out of his skin.

The burner cell phone sitting in the cup holder buzzed and rattled. Merlin glared at it, angry at the interruption.

It jangled and buzzed again.

Blowing out a small breath to calm himself, Merlin realized his nerves were getting the better of him. He was pushing hard with little sleep and it was catching up.

The buzzing and vibrating in the cup holder continued.

Sammy must have something for me. Grabbing the cell phone, Merlin was about to jab his thumb on the screen to answer it - when he froze in position.

The screen showed "private number".

That didn't make sense. He racked his brain, trying to remember back to exactly what had happened when he'd talked with Sammy before. He was tired and groggy but...no, it never showed "private number".

The cell phone insistently buzzed and vibrated in his hand.

He tapped "answer" with a thumb and put the phone to his ear, listening.

There was the sound of breathing on the other end. Steady breathing that had the air of anticipation in it. It was replaced by a familiar Parisian accent, deep in pitch, "As I told you once before, Mr. Dragon. you were foolish to remain in the city."

Merlin felt a cold shock run through his veins. The man he had assumed was the leader of those GIGN gendarmes had found him. How?

"Your compatriot has turned on you. You have no one left in support of your assignment. I advise you to give yourself up."

Glancing in the rearview mirror, Merlin wondered if they were moving in as he sat there. But there was no movement. No shadows moving in the shadows. He heard the low sounds of a few vehicles passing on the freeway to the South. But nothing else.

"Or - as a told you once before - I will find you and I will kill you–"

Ending the call, Merlin looked out at the dark, narrow street. Sammy had turned on him? He refused to believe it. Powless wasn't the type. And he wasn't just going on his own gut feeling. O'Toole had trusted her as well. They were screwing with him, playing with his head. But how did they know where he was?

And then it struck him. They didn't. At least not his exact location right now. The man had said *'you were foolish to remain in the city'*. The last time he had talked to him, Merlin was in Paris at the train station. And the last time he had talked to Sammy, he was also in the Paris area.

They had gotten to Sammy. More than likely, they had the last cell phone she had used and were able to figure out where he was when they had talked - no, she had sent him a text message. Either way, they had been able to track him several times now. But they were always one step - maybe half a step - behind him. Which meant the GIGN gendarmes were being fed the information. They weren't exactly at the spear tip of tracking him down. Why that was happening didn't make sense. But it would give Merlin some time - a day? - an hour? - there was no way of telling. But he had to push this. Moving on wasn't an option this time. The question was how? He couldn't just walk up to the front door and ask for - an idea came to him. There was something he had noticed as he looked over the renovated building. Using the night vision binoculars again, he checked the side of the house/castle. Yes, there it was. It was a dumb idea - downright idiotic at the very least - but it might just work. Do the unexpected. Setting the binoculars down, he reassembled his special cell phone to do an Internet search to find the tools he needed.

Chapter 45

AS THE SUN ROSE over Margraten Castle, Merlin pushed the van hard over the cobblestone street towards the entrance. Once he had spotted the natural gas meter on the side of the building and confirmed gas fireplaces had been installed during the renovations, he had a plan to get inside. A quick break-in on the premises of GasBedrijf, the local natural gas company, he had 'borrowed' a uniform and a van. His special Beretta was under a rumpled rag on his lap. The digital recorder was in the shirt pocket. A soft tool bag with an open top and carry handles sat on the passenger seat. It was filled with gas technician tools - wrenches, pliers, screwdrivers, wire strippers and cutters, a multimeter, a flue gas analyze,r and assorted tools. The bottom had a zippered pocket that had held small items like marettes. He had cleaned those small items out and left it unzipped.

The only way into the walled-off property on this side was through the two-story guard-house that blended into the rest of the buildings on either side of the street. Slowing the van, he turned between the two iron posts and drove through the narrow arched driveway in the middle of the guard-house. He slammed his brakes on just as he exited on the other side.

A man with a shotgun had stepped in front of the van, aiming directly at him through the windshield.

Merlin ignored the weapon, hoped his acting ability was up to the task, and frantically waved the man out of the way, yelling, "Aan de kant. Aan de kant." 'Out of the way' in Dutch. At least he hoped he was saying that. He'd used Google translate and a program that told him how to pronounce the words. For all he knew, he was using some derogatory term to swear at the guy. When he didn't move - Merlin didn't expect it - he rolled the window down quickly, waving him forward.

The guard kept the weapon up, trained on Merlin, as he moved around to the window.

Merlin spotted movement in the rearview mirror.

Another guard stepped from the guard shack behind him. His weapon - it looked like a Heckler & Koch HK433 compact assault rifle - was down but he was advancing toward the van.

Doing his best to keep an eye on both men, Merlin used his left hand to hold out the credentials he had found inside the gas company. The picture was of a beefy guy with a mustache and didn't even look like Merlin, but he just needed it to serve as a distraction. "Gevaarlijk gaslek!" he yelled to the man in front. *Dangerous gas leak.*

His eyebrows knitting together, the guard stepped forward, slightly lowering the weapon as he reached for the credentials.

Slipping his right hand under the rumpled rag, Merlin glanced in the side view mirror. The second man was near the back wheel, moving towards his partner. Slipping the Beretta from under the rag, Merlin fired at the man with the shotgun.

Crack!

The first guard's head snapped back and then he crumpled to the ground, a neat bullet hole between his eyes.

The second guard startled and brought his assault rifle up.

Merlin was a split second faster, using the rearview mirror to aim the Beretta at the man's upper torso to give him a larger target. He pulled the trigger twice.

Crack! Crack!

Dropping his weapon, the second guard clutched his chest and then fell face down.

Out of the vehicle quickly, Merlin raised his weapon with both hands and listened for the sounds of running footsteps. Everything was quiet, including the street beyond the guard shack. These appeared to be the only two guards on duty and there was little traffic this early in the morning. Grabbing each man by the collar, he pulled them away from the narrow roadway, collected their weapons and dump them beside the bodies. He retrieved the stolen credentials, got back into the van and headed for the castle. Halfway up the narrow, tree-lined entrance road, he began honking the horn. Rather than approach the next set of guards quietly, he wanted to set up the scene of a workman rushing to a frantic situation.

Two guards popped out the large front entrance, both of them with handguns, held up in two hands in combat style as they moved down the steps.

The castle was large and imposing, looming over him as he jammed on the brakes and slid to a stop. The Beretta was useless at this point and he quickly slipped it into the bottom compartment of the tool bag and zippered it closed, letting the seams close over it. Unless they looked very close, he doubted they would see the compartment. And hopefully, his frantic acting job would keep them from giving it that close look. He threw open the passenger door and jumped out, gesturing to the house/castle, "Gevaarlijk gaslek!"

The two men separated to ten feet apart and advanced on the van. The one on the left gestured for Merlin to raise his hands, "Handen omhoog. Niet bewegen."

Merlin knew he would have to drop the pretense of being a Dutchman eventually and he used an English accent as he raised his left hand over his head, "Do you speak English? I have to get in there, mate. Gevaarlijk gaslek." The European Union without borders allowed people to move across the different countries. He hoped they would buy it.

"What are you talking about? We never reported a gas leak." The man's accent was heavy but clear enough to understand.

The men on the right reached forward and pulled the soft tool bag from Merlin's hand. The tools and other items clattered as he dropped it to the ground and began to push them around, looking for weapons.

Merlin glanced at him while keeping the left hand up, "Careful there, mate. You might damage some of the gauges." He looked at the other men, "We've had a pressure increase in the lines in this area. The extra pressure is causing leaks - like in gas fireplaces? We're not sure what's causing it but some of the other technicians are checking out the other buildings. I need to get in there right now."

The man searching the soft tool bag moved around Merlin and began patting him down, "We didn't hear anything from Dolf and Gerard at the guard shack. How did you get through?"

"Get through?" Merlin shrugged, "I drove through that building at the front. I didn't see anybody."

Finding the digital recorder in the shirt pocket, the guard rolled around in his hands.

Merlin reached for it, "I need that to take notes for my report. Look, mate, I got to get in there or we all go boom. You get it?"

Letting Merlin take the recorder from his hand, he glanced to his partner.

The man on the left cursed under his breath. Then he gave a nod and gestured to the tools, "We will take you in."

Grabbing the handles on the soft tool bag, Merlin followed the man into the house as the second man lingered near the van, watching down the entrance road. The foyer was colorful and stunning, open to the second floor. Up ahead was a grand staircase that swept upward. Merlin ignored it all, "Where's the first fireplace?"

"Through here." The guard strode across the wide foyer into the hallway and turned left into a study.

Following the guard into the room, Merlin saw a fireplace on the far side. The rest of the study was lined with books in a room that also rose two stories. Several movable ladders rose to a balcony that circled the upper floor, allowing someone to access that level of the books. Several easy chairs sat off to the left. Striding to the fireplace, Merlin set the tool bag on the floor and knelt down. He discreetly turned the recorder on, intending to pull the Beretta from the hidden compartment on the tool bag and gain the advantage now that he was inside–

A gun barrel pressed against the back of his neck.

Merlin froze in position, "What's up, mate? We already went through this–"

"Do you think we are that stupid, Mr. Dragon?"

The voice came from off to the left, in the area of the easy chairs.

Slowly turning his head to look, Merlin saw one of the chairs swivel around.

A middle-aged man with graying sandy hair sat in the chair, his legs crossed and his hands holding a book. The smile was both contemptuous and smug, "I have waited for this moment for some time."

It had been some time since Merlin had last looked at the man's picture on Bonaire, but he knew who it was. "Dirk VanDaele"

The man's smile turned to one of anger and his words were sharp, "That is pronounced VanDaele. But then again, a man whose plan was so stupid, would not know any better than that, would he?"

"I guess not, *VanDaele*." Merlin made sure to butcher the name even more. He shook his head, "You use a Russian nerve agent on Director Aubrey Laurent and Evelyn O'Toole just to lure me here?"

The words the arms dealer shot back were harder and more bitter, "No. I wanted them both dead. It was payback for interfering in my business. You are - what is the expression? - the icing on the cake. It was you - *you* - who crippled our bank - who attacked my compound with some stupid makeshift bomb." He gave a dismissive shrug, "I recognize you were only doing your job, but you still wreaked havoc on our business. That is unforgivable."

Merlin realized the weapon was no longer pressed against the back of his head, and that the guard had moved back. Slowly standing up, Merlin faced VanDaele. He tried to find some way to get either man to react or overreact and allow him an opportunity to fight back. He glanced at the guard, "Your two guards at the entrance failed to stop me, VanDaele. Is this guy any better? I mean, you seem to hire failures. Like the two assassins you hired who couldn't kill Laurent or O'Toole...or me?"

VanDaele raised an eyebrow, considering Merlin for a minute. Then he burst into laughter.

So did the guard.

Merlin could only stand there in confusion, looking from one laughing man to the other, watching them exchanged looks of delight at some unknown secret.

Wiping a hand under his nose, VanDaele let out a sigh, "You really are a stupid man. There is only one assassin. We *told* the French authorities there were *two*...a man and a woman...in the hopes they would track you down and kill you. And if they didn't, well, here you are."

The laughter broke out again as Merlin stood there, stunned.

Chapter 46

THE CASTLE'S DUNGEON had been turned into a wine tasting room. Dozens of kegs were lined up on a heavy wooden rack along one wall. A heavy wooden table sat in the middle of the stone floor, surrounded by eight wooden chairs. Place settings, including several wine glasses, decorated the table. Recessed lighting set in the stone ceiling cast a soft, gentle glow over everything, including the ancient prisoner chains that still hung from the stone walls. The smell of wine and some type of cheese hung on the air.

Several other armed guards carrying Heckler & Koch MP5 submachine guns had shown up, forming an escort into the bowels of the castle and they now stood between Merlin and the door.

Merlin turned in a circle, taking in his new surroundings, looking for windows or escape points.

Dirk VanDaele stepped into the dungeon and gestured to the table, issuing instructions to his men, "Take all of the place settings away. We don't want to leave our guest with any types of weapons."

Turning to face the arms dealer, Merlin said, "You have a strange way of taking care of your guests." He gestured to the chains on the walls, "Are those for your girlfriends? I imagine that's the only way you can get any."

As three of the guards cleared away the table and carried the items, including the chairs, out of the dungeon, VanDaele glared at Merlin, "You think you are a funny man. What you are is a stupid man."

"You've already said that."

"I knew you would pull a stupid stunt like trying to get in here dressed as a gas serviceman. I know people. I hire people and I know you. You are so dedicated to doing your tasks that you will do the stupidest things to accomplish them. Your dedication is your downfall."

Merlin felt his cheeks flush.

Now VanDaele bared his teeth and scowled, "I could have my men kill you right now. But I don't want to do that. I want you to suffer. I want you to know that I *will* track down and kill your Laurent and O'Toole. Only *then* will I kill *you*."

Another guard appeared in the doorway behind VanDaele and leaned close to the arms dealer's head, whispering something.

VanDaele's face flickered with anger, he nodded once and turned, slipping past the guard and disappearing.

The guard now took up the glaring look at Merlin as his comrades passed him, following their boss.

Once they all filed out, the ancient dungeon door slammed shut with a loud boom that echoed off the stone walls and ceiling, leaving Merlin alone. *I will track down and kill your Laurent and O'Toole?* The arms dealer didn't know where they were. That was why he had crossed paths with the assassin in Tours, France. There could be all kinds of reasons for the arms dealer not knowing but Merlin pushed that from his mind. He had to concentrate on staying in between them and VanDaele's men and the assassin. For that, he needed to get out of here. Moving quickly to the heavy dungeon door, Merlin knelt and examined the lock. It looked ancient but was actually made to look like that. It was a simple tumbler lock. With the dungeon turned into a wine tasting room, there was no reason to have something more exotic or difficult for a lock picking expert. Merlin wasn't an expert yet but he was getting better. As he dug his lock picking tools from the webbing of his belt, he leaned his ear against the door and listened. It was made from heavy, thick timbers and it was difficult - if not impossible - to hear if someone was on the other side. He had to assume there were one if not two guards.

But instead of picking the lock, he stood up and stepped back from the door. If he opened the door and there were two guards, what chance did he have? He could fight, yes. But would he be able to incapacitate both men before they could react? This was different than the two gendarmes in the elevator, a tight space. The odds were against him - especially if they were a couple who carried the submachine guns - and all he would do is reveal himself and his abilities to escape a situation like this. They would confiscate his tools and he would be done.

He looked around the dungeon again, looking for a way out, looking for something that he could use. He walked to the table and ran his hand over the wood, looking underneath. The table was well-built and heavy, with strong dado joints and dowel pins used in the construction of the table. There was no way he could pull it apart with his bare hands to create a makeshift club.

Next, he checked the wine rack holding the kegs. The base and the X-beams holding the kegs in place were heavy and well-built as well. There was no way he could pull it apart. Frustrated, he put his hands on his hips and looked up, examined the stone ceiling and the recessed lights. He looked for the light switches, wondering if he could use the electrical wires against the door to electrocute someone on the other side. But there were no switches. They had to be all outside the room. And it was a dumb idea anyway.

He moved across the stone floor and tried to pull the prisoner chains out of the wall. He placed both feet against the wall and pulled hard but still couldn't budge them. Slamming them against the wall, he turned his attention to the door again as they rattled and clanked. The only thing he could do was pick the lock and try to take them by surprise. Unless, of course, he could find some way to make them open the door, and then take them by surprise. It was a slight difference, but one that could make all the difference in the world to his survival. And the survival of Laurent and O'Toole.

He turned his attention to the kegs of wine. He pushed against the bottom of one with both hands, testing its weight. Somewhere around sixty to seventy pounds. Running his hand over the curved, wooden slats and the four metal bands, he decided his plan might work. But good fortune would have to smile on him - something that seemed to have eluded him to this point. Wrestling a keg of Cabernet Sauvignon from its X-bed, he carried it across to the table. The wine moved back and forth in the wooden container and made handling it difficult. One hand lost its grip as he lowered the keg to the table and it banged hard, the sound echoing off the stone walls. He froze and listened.

There was no reaction from the guards. No one opened the door and came in.

He let out his breath. He would have to be more careful until he was ready.

The next one was a keg of Chardonnay. The variety didn't really matter. It was more a case of his heightened senses noticing every little detail. Lives were at stake. He carried the Chardonnay to within twenty feet of the door and carefully lowered it, setting the keg on its side on the stone floor. It rocked slightly as the wine sloshed back and forth. He set two more kegs on the floor behind the first, lining up all three with the dungeon door.

He was ready to put his plan into effect. But as he climbed on the wooden table, he wondered if VanDaele was right. He had a drive to fulfill whatever task was given him - but that drive could lead him to do some foolish things. And this just might be one of them.

Chapter 47

GRIPPING THE EDGES of the keg of wine, Merlin jerked the sixty pounds from the table to his waist. His body protested, his back muscles especially grieving from the pounding they had taken when the van had rolled over. Gathering his sore legs under him, Merlin grit his teeth and thrust the keg upward over his head. The grazed bullet wound screamed in its own walk of protest. Shuffling his feet forward to the edge of the table, Merlin fought the keep the barrel over his head as the wine began to move around. The moment of truth. Would it work?

Letting his arms tip forward, Merlin Let the barrel slip from his fingers.

The keg of wine dropped to the stone floor. It hit with a resounding bang off the stone walls. A split second later it burst apart, wooden slats, metal rings, and dark, rich ruby red wine exploding in all directions.

Ignoring the wine that splashed over his shoes, Merlin jumped to the floor. His feet slipped on the wet stone and went out from under him. He landed hard on his side and cursed.

A muffled shout came from the other side of the thick dungeon door.

Scrambling to his feet, Merlin flapped his hands, shedding red wine in a shower. He had to move carefully on the slick floor, amid the debris of wine keg. He couldn't afford to slip again. Reaching the three kegs, he heard the sound of a key in the door. He cursed again. He was moving too slow and time was running out. Setting his hands against the last keg, he pushed. It barely budged. Lined up one behind the other, the combined weight was close to three hundred pounds. He cursed his stupidity - maybe he should have used two - he decided to change tactics. One knee on the keg, he leaned forward and pushed on the first keg. It moved and rolled. He pushed the second keg and it did the same. Closing his eyes, he set his hands against the last keg and pushed with all his might. It slammed against the second. His feet slipped on the slick floor but Merlin persisted, slapping his hands against the last keg, pushing harder as all three rolled and gained momentum.

The door was beginning to open.

A low rumble now sounded from the three rolling kegs.

Merlin moved to the left, his feet slipping and sliding as he grabbed a wet metal ring with his left and a curved barrel slat with his right.

As the heavy door swung open, a guard appeared in the doorway, his submachine gun held in one hand and a scowl on his face as he moved forward to see what was going on inside the dungeon, "Wat ben je–?"

The rumble of the barrels echoed into the hallway.

Merlin ran to the left and just behind the rolling kegs, staying low.

His scowl turning to surprise, the guard's next reaction was to jump. But he was a fraction of a second too slow and the first rolling keg caught his foot. Grunting in protest, he slammed face down into the rolling kegs. His weapon struck the edge of the doorway, bounced off a keg and clattered to the stone floor.

The kegs continued rolling through the doorway, carrying the struggling guard on top of them.

A second guard had stepped to the side, barely pulling his leg back in time and avoiding the rolling kegs.

Merlin kept running, using the second guard's momentary hesitation to fling the metal ring backhanded.

As the second guard turned his attention back to the onrushing prisoner, he reacted by bringing his weapon up - and then flinched as the flying object struck him in the face.

Pushing the barrel of the submachine gun downward with his left, Merlin swung hard with his right.

The wooden slat caught the guard on the temple and he crumpled, unconscious, his weapon noisily bouncing off the stone floor.

Merlin kept moving, snatching up the submachine gun, he went after the first guard as the barrels came to a stop. Flipping the weapon around, he slammed the butt of the weapon into the guard's head, knocking him out. Flipping it back around, he brought it up in a combat stance, listening.

There were no other sounds. No shouts of alarm. No onrushing feet.

Turning his attention back to the two guards, he hauled them inside the dungeon, his back muscles still protesting under the weight of handling the unconscious bodies. Retrieving the other weapon, Merlin closed the dungeon door and moved down the stone hallway to the far end where he turned his attention to the narrow stairs leading upward.

He listened carefully.

There were no sounds.

Merlin knew what he would find up there. At the top of the narrow stone stairs was a large open room with a fireplace and a number of comfortable chairs and a long sofa. A large liquor cabinet and thermoelectric cigar humidor, big enough to hold two hundred cigars sat against the far wall. He assumed it was a place to entertain guests and he doubted any men would be up there.

But he couldn't be sure.

There were no voices or footsteps.

Yet...once he started up, he was at a disadvantage.

Merlin pushed the thought from his mind.

He had no choice.

Slinging one submachine gun over his good shoulder, he brought the other one up in both hands as he whispered - and he made sure he butchered the name as he began to climb, "Here I come again, VanDaele."

Chapter 48

REACHING THE TOP STEP, Merlin stepped into the open room quickly, sweeping the weapon, expecting a deadly firefight. Instead, he found a quiet room, the scent of cognac the only evidence someone had been in here. The covered terrace beyond the glass patio doors on the left was empty. Low voices could be heard through the open doorway up ahead and just to the right. Finger on the trigger, weapon against his shoulder, Merlin advanced across the room at an angle that put him against the left door frame. He visualized the details of the hallway that ran left and right on the other side. It actually circled a large games room across from this one. He had noticed a pool table at dartboard when they had marched him to the repurposed dungeon. Beyond that was a large room that was open to the second floor. The staircase was off to the left. He checked the hallway to the right from this side, peered around the door frame, and then darted across to check the other side of the hallway. He didn't see anyone and the voices appeared to be moving to the room open to the second floor.

A surprise attack was all he had from here. Even with two machine guns, it was unlikely he would survive. He decided neither side, and especially the arms dealer, should survive if it came to that. Backing away from the doorway, he moved across the room to the gas fireplace. Dropping the access panel at the bottom, he used the butt of his weapon to strike against the control valve. He did it twice and listened for anyone coming down the hall. There were no footsteps headed this way and so he banged once more against the control valve, knocking it off this time. It only took a few seconds for the rotten egg smell to rise from the damaged control.

Slipping the second submachine gun from his shoulder, Merlin now moved to the open doorway with the weapon in each hand. He slipped through, moved to the right side of the hall, placed his back against the wall and listened. He could hear the voices but he wasn't totally positive where they were now. He considered a low advance around the hallway and then changed tactics. Slipping to the other side of the hallway, and moved to the entrance of the games room and peered inside. It was empty. Slipping into the room, he used the central pool table as cover as he moved forward across the room, trying to keep half his attention on the doorway behind him as well.

The voices seem to be moving off to the left.

Circling around to the other side of the pool table, Merlin moved sideways to the door, always cognizant that the attack could come from behind as well. Pressing himself against the plaster wall in the right side of the doorway, Merlin listened.

The voices were definitely moving off to the left.

To Merlin, it sounded like they were headed to the front entrance. Now afraid he could lose VanDaele, Merlin knew he had to act. But he also knew he had the stack the odds of taking out the arms dealer in his favor. He moved across to the gas fireplace servicing this room and quickly knocked out the control valve. He could smell the gas filling the room as he moved back to the doorway and prepared himself.

A submachine gun in both hands, Merlin took a deep breath and left the games room. He moved as quickly as he could towards the front entrance.

Six armed men stood near the open front entrance. They were conversing in low tones.

Merlin didn't see VanDaele and he cursed himself. Maybe taking that extra moment to knock out the valve on the gas fireplace had allowed the arms dealer to get into a car and drive away. Feeling his rage build at missing his target, Merlin took off at a run, using that rage to let out a battle cry.

The six men were startled. The immediately turned, trying to bring their weapon off their shoulder or to bring it up into firing position.

Pulling the trigger on both submachine guns, Merlin yelled at the top of his lungs as the slugs ripped through the men.

They jerked in a macabre dance of death.

As the bodies and weapons dropped to the stone floor, Merlin jumped into the open doorway, looking for the arms dealer.

The two men who had stopped him earlier were rushing from the van to the castle.

Merlin pulled the triggers again, taking down both men. When he stopped firing, everything went quiet. The smell of gunfire hung heavy in the air. Where was–?

Running footsteps sounded off somewhere behind him.

Turning around on his heels, Merlin lifted both weapons, ready for an attack.

It never came.

The footsteps were actually running away inside the castle. It had to be VanDaele.

Merlin closed the front door and locked it to slow any more men arriving. Then he took off at a run, throwing caution to the wind. The arms dealer knew his own castle better than Merlin, and if he lost him in the maze of rooms, he may not have the time to find him before reinforcements arrived. Trying to stay alert to an attack from any doorway or hallway as he ran, Merlin tried to keep his own footsteps as light as possible so he could hear where the person fleeing was going.

He could tell he was closing in. And then his heart skipped a beat when the sound of the running disappeared. A moment later, he skidded to a stop. Across a large open room was a set of glass doors leading to a large patio outside the back of the castle. And no VanDaele. No –

A boom sounded off to the left that indicated a heavy door was banged shut.

Merlin took off at a run, passed through an open archway, turned to his right - and came face-to-face with a heavy, metal door.

A square window in the door framed the smug face of Dirk VanDaele.

Merlin watched him bend slightly to the right, and then the face reappeared. A speaker somewhere above him carried the Dutch-accented voice of the arms dealer.

"Like I said, Mr. Dragon, you are a stupid man. You may have killed my men, but there are already more on the way." His smile broadened, "This is my safe room, the bulletproof glass and the thick, reinforced walls are impenetrable by you and the weapons you now carry. Of course, you could retrieve heavy, industrial equipment or enough explosives to penetrate the door. But by the time you do - well - you won't have that time. My men *will* kill you. The only sad thing is, I won't be able to tell you when I have killed Laurent and O'Toole."

Merlin slowly lowered both weapons as he stared into the eyes of the arms dealer. Checkmate.

Chapter 49

OR MAYBE IT WAS ONLY CHECK. And not checkmate. Moving away from the door, he ran a hand along the plaster wall, considering the weak points in a safe room. The safe room was built in the back left corner of the castle. It was using the left and back castle walls of thick stone to limit the possible penetration to the front and right wall of the safe room. The arms dealer had renovated the insides of the castle so Merlin didn't have to deal with stone. But even plaster walls could be reinforced on the inside with concrete. Or perhaps steel plating. And with a steel door, VanDaele was right, there was no way he could break through any of the walls. Time was running out again but he forced himself to close his eyes and think. An idea came to him and he moved back to the small window. He didn't see the arms dealer's face this time and he looked inside the safe room.

VanDaele was in the middle of the room now, a satellite phone to his ear. No doubt it was hooked into an antenna on the roof and he was calling for added reinforcements.

Merlin did his best to scan the interior of the safe room with his limited scope of view through the foot square window. He spotted what he felt would work and estimated the distances from the back and right wall to be about three feet. Scanning the room again for any other possibilities, he decided it was all he had. Hoping he had the time needed, he worked his way back to the stairs. Weapon up, just in case, Merlin climbed the wide staircase and made his way to the back left side of the castle. The area above the safe room below was covered by a large bedroom that seemed longer but was the same width. He went to the back right corner and paced off three feet along the right wall. He couldn't see a reason why this wall would be reinforced. At least he hoped not.

Taking a step back, Merlin raised the submachine gun and began firing into the plaster wall. Dust and debris exploded into the air. He kept on firing, digging a hole in the wall until he spotted what he needed.

VanDaele had a positive pressure air filtration system in the safe room below. It used a HEPA filter and an activated carbon filter. to protect against the many gases, vapors, and aerosols that could be released in an accident or terrorist act. In addition, the unit created positive air pressure inside the safe room so that all air was going out. But it also had an intake pipe and an exhaust pipe. And that's what he had found. The bullets had punctured both pipes but the important one was the intake pipe - it was used to draw air into the safe room where it was filtered. Next, he turned his attention to the fireplace, knocking out the valve. The smell of rotten eggs began to fill the room - the sign natural gas was being released. One of his old army bases had used natural gas vehicles for the short runs around the base and he had learned to service them in a pinch. And he had learned that natural gas is primarily composed of methane, a colorless, odorless, non-toxic flammable gas that can create a massive explosion. But methane wasn't just dangerous - it had an extremely low molecular weight and that made it unfilterable. VanDaele's intake pipe for the filtration system below would be sucking in the natural gas.

Making his way back downstairs - the smell of rotten eggs from his earlier work was now very evident - and he headed straight for the study. He found the tool bag still on the floor where he had left it. He retrieved the recorder - it was still running and he turned it off - and his Beretta. He slipped that into his waistband and headed for the desk where he searched for a lighter or matches. He cursed under his breath when he didn't find anything. He had something in his belt that would work to create a spark but it was going to take time–

Banging and pounding came from the front entrance.

Merlin stepped out of the study quickly.

More of VanDaele's men had arrived and were trying to break down the front door.

Time had run out and Merlin darted for the back of the castle.

A loud crash sounded, indicating the men had breached the front entrance.

Weaving his way towards those patio doors, Merlin's mind whirled, looking for some way to finish what he had come to do. The problem was, he couldn't get to the arms dealer and he couldn't find a way to – shouts came from behind him. They were chasing his running footsteps, just as he had done with VanDaele.

Reaching the large back room, Merlin darted across the floor. And then a thought struck him. What if the doors are locked? He had no choice. He raised the submachine gun as he ran, pulled the trigger and shattered the glass–

The natural gas filling the castle exploded.

Every window and doorway was blown outward and shattered into a million pieces of molten sand and burning wood.

A black and orange ball of flame smashed into Merlin's back and enveloped him in a smothering cocoon of pain.

Chapter 50

MERLIN DRAGON LANDED HARD. And instinctively rolled. His clothing was on fire. He left a trail of smoke and burning embers along the angel stone patio, came to a stop on his left side and then everything faded. A sudden intake of breath took him into a place of panic and he rolled over, hands slapping for something. A weapon. He needed a weapon. Why? He wasn't sure – the raging fire to his left brought it all back. He rolled over to his butt and groaned from the effort as he looked for a weapon again. A submachine gun lay ten feet in front of him and he rolled to his knees. Moving slowly across the patio on his hands and knees - he knew he had to move faster but his body protested - he finally laid a hand on the weapon. Cradling it, he rolled over to his butt again, looking back at the fire. The flames roared, tongues of orange licking through every opening at the stone walls, blackening them. There was no one in pursuit.

Spotting his special Beretta, Merlin gingerly got to his feet, retrieved it and began limp-walking away from the scene, intending to go through the back fields. That was going to take forever and he doubted he would get far. So he changed tactics, forcing himself to move faster around the castle to the front. He had to skirt wide around the ruins of an old lookout tower and by the time he reached the front left corner he could see a number of townspeople were on-scene, pointing and discussing the burning castle. The sounds of a siren coming up the tree-lined driveway announced the arrival of the fire department - two fire engines actually. It was too late to make an unseen getaway. Or maybe not.

Merlin could see there were several large SUVs parked haphazardly next to the GasBedrijf van he had stolen. The doors were wide open on two of them, more than likely the vehicles VanDaele's men and used to get here. If he could get to one of them, he might be able to make a discrete getaway yet. He began limping toward the cluster of vehicles and then realized he was still carrying the submachine gun and the Beretta. He slipped back behind the ruins, wiped his prints from the submachine gun - they were probably all over everything inside anyway - and tossed it to the ground. He couldn't rip away the gas company logo from the shirt - it was sown into the fabric - and so he simply took the shirt off, turned it inside out and put it back on again, keeping it untucked to cover the Beretta in his waistband. He had to hope no one paid any attention in the chaos as the fire engines began to battle the blaze. Again moving wide to his left, Merlin eventually came up behind the vehicles and the crowds eying the ancient burning structure. A few more vehicles were coming to a stop, parking here and there, but no one paid the least bit of attention to him as he slipped into the open passenger door of an SUV. He closed the door closed and slid across to the other side, relieved to find a set of keys hanging from the ignition. Pulling the driver side door closed, he eyed the crowd as he started the engine. Again, no one paid any attention to him. He paused for a moment, looking at the burning structure, orange flames and a cloud of black smoke climbing into the early morning sky. If VanDaele had survived - and he doubted it - he would have to try again sometime down the road. Right now, he had someone else to see. Backing the SUV into a turn, he drove away, taking a path along the grass outside the entrance road is another fire engine bellowed its way to the scene.

Chapter 51

LYON, FRANCE

THE FLIGHT ITSELF was under two hours. But every dip or bump from air turbulence made it seem like an eternity for Merlin. Captain Faith Saab had put her field dressing expertise to work, cleaning and bandaging the nicks and cuts that he couldn't reach himself. He had literally bathed himself with several bottles of muscle liniment but the relief wasn't going to come for a few days. In fact, the discomfort was probably going to increase. Because he had to keep pushing himself. There was no time to rest and heal.

It was nearing midnight and Merlin Dragon now stood in the Presqu'ile quarter, the heart of Lyon, leaning to one side to try and offset the back spasms, looking up at the soft lights of one particular apartment in the fancy ten-story building. He had used his special cell phone hooked into Interpol's 24-7 databases and found the man's itinerary. He had hosted a small dinner party for five others. Merlin had watched his guests leave twenty minutes ago and he waited to see if there were any others. There weren't and he decided it was time. Actually, there was little time. He still had no idea where the assassin was. He doubted there would be any guards, but he double-checked his

Beretta, just in case. And then he patted his shirt pocket, ensuring the black, carbon fiber pen was there.

Jogging across the quiet street, Merlin pulled his lock picking tools from his belt. He was dressed completely in black, including a black ball cap, and felt like a ninja. Actually, with all the sore muscles, bruises, nicks, and cuts, the way he moved was like a poor man's ninja. The foyer was empty and Merlin went to work on the entrance door. It took nearly a minute but finally opened and Merlin slipped inside, slipping the tools into his back pocket. He kept his head down and turned away from the security cameras as he crossed to the elevator. Pulling the cap low to avoid the security cameras inside the elevator, Merlin punched the button for the top floor and the penthouse. The elevator rose smoothly, finally came to a stop, and the doors whispered open. This time, Merlin stuffed the cap in his left pocket before pulling a balaclava from his right and slipping it over his head. Punching the emergency stop button to keep the elevator in place, Merlin strolled down the hallway, took the lock picking tools in hand and went to work. He cursed softly under his breath this time. His fingers and hands were sore as well and it took well over a minute before the door unlocked. He replaced the tools with the Beretta and he hoped his aching fingers didn't become a detriment. Slipping inside the apartment, Merlin closed the door softly. The room was large and open, with a long sofa, several easy chairs, a coffee table, a liquor cabinet, and another cabinet with some kind of crystal collection. Expensive looking art lined the walls. As he moved slowly across the cork flooring, the scents of wine and cheese reminded him of the dungeon and his muscles tensed He wiggled the fingers in his free hand, trying to lessen the tension as he listened carefully for any–

Footsteps came from the left.

Merlin lifted the weapon with both hands and turned.

A tall, sandy-haired man with hard blue eyes appeared. He wore a fancy three-piece suit that was without the jacket right now. A Rolex watch adorned one wrist, some fancy signet ring announced its significance and association with the expensive cufflinks. The startled look on the man's face was quickly replaced by one of anger and he spoke in his native tongue, "Vem är du? Och vad gör du här? Vet du–?"

"Shut up. And move over there." Merlin indicated with the gun for him to move to the long white sofa on his right.

The man's eyebrows pushed hard together and he stood stubbornly in place, "Do you know who I am and what will happen–?"

"Yeah. You're Tuur Peeters, a slimy politician that I should shoot just on principle. Oh...and you're also Interpol's Secretary-General...and that's the only reason I'm going to give you another chance to move to the sofa. Now do it."

Peeters hesitated, turned his head slightly, his eyes indicating he was considering the hallway behind him.

"Don't do anything stupid."

It took a few more seconds but Peeters grudgingly complied and trudged his way across the floor, his face a mask of anger. He sat down, his voice hard, "Take whatever you want and go."

"I'm the one giving the orders–"

Footsteps and a voice came from the hallway, "I'm very sorry, Tuur, I didn't mean to–"

Merlin swung the weapon in the direction of the voice. And he cursed inside. He wasn't expecting this.

A beautiful, dark-haired woman dressed in a black form-fitting, knee-length dress stood frozen in the hallway. Her head was tilted to the right, her hand pushing aside her hair and still on the earring she was working on. Her dark eyes focused on the balaclava.

Gesturing with his Beretta, Merlin instructed the woman to, "Keep coming. I want you to sit beside your boyfriend." Like Peeters, she hesitated a moment and he told her, "Hurry up."

The woman did as she was told, her stilettos clicking across the floor to the sofa. She took up a spot beside Peeters. bent her head toward him and whispered, "What's going on?"

Peeters patted her on the knee, "Don't you worry about it. He won't do anything to you. I'll make sure of that." He glared up at Merlin, "And she's not my girlfriend. Stefana Lazar is Interpol's General Secretariat. She manages the day-to-day operation under my direction.

Merlin noted the familiar touch of his hand on her bare knee. He didn't like the guy already and now it looked like he was lying, "Is that the only thing she does under you?"

His lips curling, Peeters snarled, "If you didn't have that weapon–"

Lazar returned the familiar pat on the knee and then flicked back the hair from the side of her face, "It is all right, Tuur. Nothing he says can hurt me."

The gesture allowed Merlin to see a bruise on her right temple. His anger rose and he looked back at Peeters. *She had been apologizing for doing something. Did he beat her when he made him angry?* Merlin wanted to fill him full of holes right now.

Peeters glared right back, "I want you to take whatever you want and leave–"

"Shut - up." Merlin pulled the digital recorder from his pocket, took a step and set it down on the glass coffee table. He would get his answers *and* she would know who he was. Turning on the recorder, he stepped back to watch his reactions

Peeters' brows knit together as the recorded conversations started, "What is this?"

"Shut your mouth and listen."

This time he scowled. And he continued that look until the voice of Larz Vermeeg sounded from the recorder. Then his eyebrows flickered.

Lazar cocked her head, "Tuur? Isn't that–?"

Peeters raised a hand to silence her.

The General Secretariat pursed her lips and placed her hands on her knees

As the conversation continued, Merlin noticed the politician's expression changed to one of concern. Then to one of anger. Then to one of embarrassment.

Lazar raised an eyebrow but didn't look at Peeters, "Tuur, is what he is saying–?

Peeters raised a hand to silence her and he glared at Merlin's eyes, growling, "That doesn't mean anything–"

Merlin glared right back, "You were being played and you know it. Now shut up and listen."

Sulking, Peeters opened his mouth to protest and then shut it. His mouth worked to hold back the words as the next conversation began.

Taking one hand from the Beretta, Merlin flexed it, trying to get rid of the stiffness that was creeping in.

There was no doubting the reaction of Peeters when Francisca Daane's voice came from the recorder. But there was a look of fright when he heard Daane admit that she had used her political influence to get Peeters to pressure the French to back off the investigation. There was no doubt the death of his political future passed before his eyes. But he seemed to find a lifeline when Daane said it was done with the purpose of drawing out Merlin. He looked up, his eyes returning to their hardness, "*You* are this Dragon? *You* are the one who is helping Laurent to twist Interpol's mission statement into–?"

Merlin grabbed the recorder in anger and turned it off, his voice rising, "*You* talk about twisting things–?" Merlin cut himself off. A lot of the anger he was feeling was at himself. For not realizing how much he would reveal about himself as well with these conversations. Right now, Merlin wanted to kill Peeters and be done with the whole thing. But the woman wouldn't be so easy. Actually, he *wouldn't* be able to do it. She was an innocent, trapped in a situation she had nothing to do with.

Chapter 52

STEFANA LAZAR, Interpol's General Secretariat, sat watching Merlin. Her eyes were narrowed as she slipped the hem of her black, form-fitting dress back a few inches. Her fingers began tapping nervously on her bare knees.

Merlin took his eyes from the beautiful woman, stopped cursing himself and attempted to repair the damage, "Apparently, I gave you too much credit, Peeters. But I guess you're really an idiot."

Tuur Peeters bristled at the words.

"It's much easier to use *real* backgrounds like the reporter Bell and this Dragon character. I don't have to make all that stuff up. But then you're a *bureaucrat* and have no idea what real fieldwork is like."

His fingers curled into fists and Peeters glared up at Merlin.

Merlin shook his head and shrugged as he did his best to make sure the smile he put on his lips showed through the mouth oval on the balaclava, "I've always wondered if the people I've used - like Bell and Dragon - would be thrown in jail someday based on what I do." He shrugged, "I guess they just have to pay the price for protecting our democracy."

Peeters sneered, "Democracy? You spout the word but don't know anything about the meaning."

Merlin stepped forward and around the table, jabbing the gun in the politician's face, "You're the one who's giving me a lecture?" He gestured to the recorder, "You're the one who is trading political favors to stop an investigation into an attempted assassination. How is that going to go for your political career, jackass?"

Pulling his head back slightly from the gun, Peeters swallowed, "You...you can't connect me to that part of it."

Merlin stepped back and snapped the recorder on again. Holding it out in his palm, he let it play his conversation with Dirk VanDaele in the castle.

Peeters blinked and licked his lips when he heard VanDaele admit using a Russian nerve agent on Laurent and O'Toole. He opened his mouth–

"And don't think you're going to try and smooth talk me into giving you the recording." Merlin turned the recorder off, slipping it into a pocket. "This is my insurance policy. Laurent and the woman don't have anything to do with this. VanDaele fell for my undercover identities and connections."

A look of defiance on his face, Peeters shot back, "You think I'm going to buy that?"

Merlin shrugged, "I don't really care what you buy. Because if the recorder doesn't work, then *this* will." He gestured with the Beretta, his role as The Stopper coming to the forefront, "*My* bottom line mission statement is to do whatever is necessary."

Peeters swallowed as the message came across clearly. His hand moved slowly to Lazar's knee without looking away from the weapon, folding his fingers around her hand in comfort, "Don't worry. I won't let anything happen to you."

A flickering smile at his concern crossed Lazar's lips but she kept her eyes on Merlin.

Slipping his hand from Lazar, Peeters took a breath and looked up into Merlin's eyes, his words bitter, "All right. There is a reason you came here to reveal this *information* to me. Your reference to an insurance policy implies you want something in return." His lips curled, "In return for this *blackmail*."

"Call it what you want," Merlin said. "First. You've done something with this Constable Samantha Powless in your Canadian office—"

"She's a traitor. Or at the very least, she doesn't obey orders—"

Merlin's voice rose along with his anger, "That's what you're going with? You're the one who interfered with an investigation at the request of a fellow politician. Remember? The Constable was doing her duty, ignoring the request she knew was wrong to find and help two members of Interpol. The organization *you* are supposed to lead."

Peeters' face hardened, "And *another* constable is dead because of her."

"Because he was aggressively pursuing someone he was told was passing information to Russian agents. An accusation against Samantha Powless that is *false*. I wonder where that idea came from?"

His face now looked conflicted.

"And sending someone to kill Powless before that—"

Scowling this time, Peeters said, "I have no idea what you're talking about."

Merlin was tired of the cat and mouse conversation, "Fine. Once the news media gets wind of this, they can do a deep dive investigation into the whole thing."

Peeters raised his hand in protest, "Now hold on, we had a deal—"

"No. I had a deal. You don't have anything. *You* just do what you're told, get it?"

Every muscle in his face twitched as Peeters fought to hold his tongue. A few moments later he nodded, "Fine. I'll make a call."

"You make sure you do. Second, I need to find Laurent and O'Toole. The assassin hired by VanDaele is still on the job—"

"Yes, I know. And they are safe," Peeters said. "I used the French National Gendarmerie to make sure they were taken to a hospital equipped to handle the nerve agent and where they could be guarded."

"That was you?" That made sense to Merlin. VanDaele fed the information to Peeters, who passed it to the guy in Paris who was trying to kill him. That's why he was always a step behind. Merlin nodded to himself, "Good. So they *are* in Dublin, Ireland."

That startled Peeters, "How did you know–?"

"It's my job to know these things. I also need you to tell that guy who's leading the French National team to back off. He keeps trying to track me down and kill me. I need to focus on the assassin before–"

"Phillipe Leneave?" Peeters shook his head, "No, it's not possible. I have never spoken with the Colonel. I made arrangements through General Garon Janvier, the General Director of the National Gendarmerie."

"Then tell this Janvier to have his man back off."

Peeters huffed, "And I'm saying Colonel Leneave would never do that. And General Janvier would *never* have his men act that way." He looked to the woman, "Tell him, Stefana. I was at the General Assembly meeting and you were the one who coordinated all the day-to-day interaction–" Peeters froze.

Stefana Lazar merely looked back at him, pursing her lips, hands still on her bare knees.

His jaw worked silently for a moment before Peeters added, "You...you were not in the office...."

"Of course I was," Lazar said.

Peeters shook his head, "No. We spoke by phone. But at one point I couldn't get you and I called your office. I was told you had been away for a full day and I contacted your assistant to handle a matter–" His eyes narrowing, Peeters said, "You were recommended for the job by Dirk VanDaele."

In an instant, it all came home to Merlin. The bruise on Stefana Lazar's face now made sense - the fight in the Chru Hôpitaux De Tours. And why those gendarmes were always one step behind - she needed the time gap to finish the job and/or kill him - maybe she even followed him, used him, trying to find Laurent and O'Toole. It didn't mattter. Because now he also knew who had access to worldwide criminal databases connected to Interpol and who reached to hire someone to kill Sammy. He looked to the woman–

She was on the coffee table and the black form-fitting dress had been pulled up to the top of her thighs. Her long, bare legs flashed.

Merlin grunted as her right foot struck his hand.

The Beretta clattered to the floor.

Lazar spun around on the table, her bare legs flashing in a roundhouse kick.

Instinctively Merlin brought his arm up. Her left leg smashed powerfully into his forearm, driving it back into his head. A sharp blow struck Merlin's temple and the room whirled. A helpless moment later, his face slammed into the floor and Merlin fought off the blackness.

Chapter 53

THROUGH THE DARK FOG that clouded his vision, Merlin saw Tuur Peeters scrambling backward like a crab on his butt. Bare feet stalked the politician, moving this way and that, trying to corner him against a large easy chair that blocked his escape.

Peeters rolled away, grabbed the leg of a wooden chair and threw it along the floor at the bare feet.

The feet jumped.

The chair banged and bounced away somewhere.

Without a sound, the feet came back down to the floor.

Peeters rolled again.

A black spike struck the floor where he had been.

Merlin was confused at what he was seeing and struggled to turn and lift his head just a few inches. The woman's bare legs and black dress around her upper thighs came into his view.

Stefana Lazar was moving in a practiced, low crouch toward the politician. Her hands held two black objects.

It was her stilettos. Lazar was using them as weapons, one in each hand.

There was a warm, wet feeling on his temple and Merlin touched the area with his fingers. The material on the balaclava had a small, horseshoe-shaped cut in it and Merlin nearly puked. His mind flashed back to a high school physics class. The teacher had them all laughing when he showed how the narrow heel on a woman's stilettos created more pressure on a floor than an elephant's foot. Only it wasn't so funny right now. If he hadn't gotten his arm up on that roundhouse kick, she would've driven the heel on her stiletto into his skull. In this case, the stilettos weren't just a fashion statement, there were deadly weapons.

Peeters yelled something at Lazar, spun to his hands and knees and scrambled away.

Lazar brought one of the shoes down and the spiked heel slammed into the laminate floor.

As her bare feet moved after Peeters again, Merlin realized her strike had left a hole in the flooring, confirming his estimate of the danger. He cursed under his breath as he brought his hands under him, trying to get up. She had been a handful in the dark hospital in Tours, what chance did he have when she had weapons in her hands?

Lazar spun around, looking in Merlin's direction. She took a step.

He knew he was in trouble and Merlin struggled harder. His hand slid out from under him and he slammed back into the floor, groaning from the blow that took away his breath.

"Stop!"

Spinning back in the other direction, Lazar faced Peeters.

The politician was on his back and held Merlin's Beretta in his hands. He was aiming at Lazar, "Put...put your hands up. Or I will shoot."

Lazar took two steps, testing his resolve.

Merlin struggled to get up again. He opened his mouth, trying to warn—

"Please don't, Stefana. I don't want to hurt you. We can figure this out."

Ignoring the warning, Lazar took another step.

Peeters pulled the trigger. His eyebrows pushed together. He pulled the trigger again. Looked at the Beretta. Aimed and pulled again, again, and again.

With a laugh, Lazar took a long step and her bare foo kicked the gun from the politician's hands.

It soared, banged onto the floor and bounced away.

Lazar raised a stiletto over her head, the light glinting off the dagger heel.

Raising his hands high, Peeters emitted a weak, "No."

Merlin gathered himself. He had to do something. Shaky feet under him, he pushed his legs against the cork flooring and launched his body toward the assassin.

Lazar seemed to feel rather than hear the movement and she turned.

His shoulder slammed into her stomach and Merlin felt the hardness of her abdomen. They both slammed into the floor. Merlin heard the stilettos bounce on the floor.

Slipping an arm under Merlin's, Lazar used the leverage of his momentum and flipped him over.

Merlin flopped like a fish in the floor. He rolled and slid himself back on his butt, knowing she would be attacking.

And she was.

Lazar advanced on him, one stiletto at the ready to strike. The other was a couple of feet away.

Her black dress was hiked and Merlin took in her long legs. It reminded him of a time he was on the hallway floor after an assignment and Jaimee Hartman's robe had parted, giving him a similar view. Only this wasn't Jamie. But he did wonder if he'd ever see her again. And Jigs – he pushed the thoughts from his mind as he slid himself back on the floor. He had to concentrate with all his being or he *would* die–

A wooden chair smashed across the woman's back, splinters of wood flying in all directions.

Lazar dropped to a knee, a stunned look on her face as her free hand kept her from falling over completely.

Peeters stood over her, the remnants of the chair held in his hands. His words were barely a whisper, "I'm...I'm sorry, Stefana, you left me no...."

Blood trickled from Lazar's mouth. She wiped it away with the back of her hand and her blood-stained lips curled into a grin. Her eyes flashed and she pirouetted on the knee and struck.

Screaming at the top of his lungs, Peeters dropped to the floor, clutching his left calf. Blood poured through his fingers. He desperately began sliding back across the floor, leaving a blood trail as he tried to put distance between himself and his attacker.

Merlin saw the blood on the heel of the stiletto in her right hand. He scrambled around to his feet, taking a step to gain some distance as he pulled the only weapon he had quick access to - the carbon fiber pen. He flipped the cap off and palmed the hollow tube, the sharp point at the ready. The assassin was on her feet and facing him again as he turned, ready to fight to the death.

Lazar's eyes narrowed as she scanned the floor.

Cursing under his breath, Merlin realized she had heard the cap drop to the floor. The woman was a formidable opponent, missing nothing.

Taking several crouching steps to her left, Lazar grabbed the other stiletto. But instead of just getting up and advancing on Merlin, she took a discrete glance to make sure Peeters was staying put. When she saw him on his side in a fetal position, eyes closed, she turned her attention back to her other target. Her eyes narrowed as she slipped the stilettos back onto her feet. Then she rose slightly, pulling the dress up around her bare thighs.

Merlin saw her bloody smile and his blood ran cold. He scrambled away a few more feet, where his back slammed into the wall. Pushing against the surface, he got to his feet and held the pointed carbon fibers pen underhanded, wondering how much longer he had to live.

Chapter 54

STEFANA LAZAR MOVED in on her target, her footwork a triangular pattern, moving forward and back, left and right, looking for superior positioning.

Focusing on her waist, Merlin tried to feel rather than see–

Lazar stepped forward, spun around and her right leg shot out.

Merlin barely moved his head in time.

Her stiletto struck the wall, the heel stabbing into the plaster.

Sliding to his left, Merlin jabbed at her side with the carbon fiber weapon.

Her bare leg still in the air, Lazar slapped the attempt away and grinned at him.

Shuffling backwards and moving several feet away from the assassin, Merlin shifted his weapon underhanded, from hand-to-hand like a knife fighter.

Lazar's smile left her face and she lowered her leg back to the floor. Smoothly shifting around to face him, she began the triangular dance again, this time on a pair of makeshift daggers, her face impassive as she looked for her next opening.

And Merlin knew it was only a matter of time before she found it. Watching her movements, he tried to see a pattern. If he could guess her next set of steps–

With her hands keeping the hem of her black dress high, Lazar switched from triangular to linear footwork.

Merlin took two quick steps back, anticipating a strike. It didn't come.

A heartbeat later, Lazar took a quick hop forward and kicked upward.

Her foot slipped between Merlin's hands as he was moving his weapon from one hand to the other. The foot struck the carbon fiber pen and it was driven straight upward and buried itself in the ceiling. Merlin cursed himself. She had anticipated his anticipation. He moved back.

Dancing forward after him, Lazar faked a kick to his shins and then whirled, bringing her right stiletto around in the air.

Merlin barely moved his head in time. He heard the shoe whizz by his ear - his foot banged against the coffee table and he fell backward awkwardly, twisting and landing hard on top of it on his side.

Lazar's eyes gleamed and she jumped to the attack.

Rolling to his left, Merlin dropped to the floor.

Her deadly heel came down on the top of the coffee table, leaving a crescent-shaped gouge in the wood. Lazar growled at the near miss, turned and continued the attack.

Scrambling away, Merlin got to his feet, hands out, doing his best to deflect the kicks that came from every angle. He slammed into a wall, his head hitting a painting.

Lazar took a small hop and whirled around.

Merlin saw her leg coming around and he slid along the wall to his left in a panic.

The artwork was destroyed as her heel slashed across the trees and mountains.

Lazar slid to her right, playing cat and mouse, keeping him against the wall. Next came the obliteration of the blue water in a Mediterranean scene.

This time Merlin darted away from the wall and then backed up, trying to keep some distance. His heart skipped several beats when he backed into the liquor cabinet. The bottles and glassware rattled and clattered together. He was in trouble and he ducked, dropping to a knee.

Lazar's front thrust-kick shot over his head. The sounds of glass shattering and wood splintering filled the room. Glasses and bottles inside the cabinet shattered violently.

Merlin had his chance - he looked at his target - he hesitated - and then brought his shoulder up instinctively.

Lazar brought her arm down, striking hard in a karate chop at his jugular vein.

Only his raised shoulder saved Merlin, deflecting the blow. It slammed into his lower jaw instead. The pain was immense and he dropped to the floor and rolled away. Coming up to his feet again, Merlin grimaced and put a hand to his throbbing jawline. That's all he needed, another sore body part.

Lazar's bloody lips grinned as she watched him, calmly pulling her stiletto from the shattered cabinet. Broken wood, glass, and bottles showered the floor.

Under normal circumstances - and if his opponent had been a man in the same position with his legs open like that - Merlin would have driven a fist between her legs to incapacitate her and end the fight.

Lazar turned to face him, her words taunting, "Your mother would be so proud of you."

Merlin cursed himself, especially since Lazar's smile and words meant she knew she had made a mistake...and he had failed to take advantage of it. He put his hands in a defensive position again and circle to her left, "I was just afraid to get bitten by crabs."

The smile dropped and Lazar's eyes flashed. She pulled the dress high on her legs again and went into the triangular footwork again, advancing on Merlin.

Continuing to circle away from her, Merlin watched for an opening again, "Don't take it personally. Well, on second thought, take it personally–"

Lazar's throat emitted a growl - it increased in ferocity as she attacked with a series of kicks.

Merlin barely avoided them. The last one cut across his stomach and shredded the material of his pullover, leaving a bloody trail behind in his skin. He grimaced in pain as he continued to circle, glancing over to Peeters. The man was sitting up against the far wall, bloody hands clutching his lower leg. His face was a mask of pain as well and Merlin doubted he would be joining in the fight again.

Lazar's footwork changed to circular movement patterns.

Swearing under his breath, Merlin knew time was running out. Circular footwork was more difficult to master than the other methods but she looked completely comfortable. It was a very effective method, used to attack at an angle in order to occupy the opponent's blind spot while limiting the opponent's options for attack. Not that Merlin was attacking–

Lazar moved in fast.

A new series of kicks slammed into the sides of Merlin's legs and he barely stayed upright. His leg muscles began to cramp from the blows and he understood what she was doing. Lazar was playing it smart. She was slowing him down for the final attack and taking no chances. Their last encounter had been brief and she still had no idea what kind of close hand-to-hand combat experience he had. And his extra body weight was not something she planned on dealing with. His eyes swept the room, looking for a weapon. He spotted two possibilities, one closer than the other. A plan formed and Merlin continued circling, working towards the closest. He faked a run to his right.

Lazar moved to cut him off.

Merlin dove to the floor in the other direction, ignoring the broken glass and wooden splinters. He grimaced in pain as something sharp bit his wrist but he managed to wrap his fingers around the neck of a broken vodka bottle.

Growling at his deception, Lazar went after him - and stopped in her tracks.

Rising to his feet, blood dripping from his wrist, Merlin held the broken Smirnov bottle underhanded - he felt like an old-time cowboy in a saloon fight.

Letting go of the hem of her dress, Lazar brought her hands up in a defensive posture.

Merlin smiled at her, "Things change, don't they?"

Lazar shrugged without looking away from the jagged bottle, "You mean you have to change your diaper? I didn't mean to scare you so much."

Ignoring her jab, Merlin made one of his own with the Smirnov bottle, aiming for her stomach.

Slapping his hand to the side, Lazar thrust stiff fingers at his throat.

Merlin twisted in reaction and the blow was just enough to make him gag.

Lazar grinned and kicked. The tight dress was lower now and kept her legs from a full thrust but she still struck home.

His fingers felt like they had snapped and Merlin dropped the bottle. He heard it hit the floor as he lowered his head in a bull rush. He caught her around the waist again and drove his legs forward.

Anticipating the move, Lazar let his movement take her backward and then she dropped, using his weight to toss him up and over her rolling body.

Merlin hit the cork floor hard, his breath expelling under the force. He fought to maintain his concentration, twisted around on the floor and scrambled away from her.

Lazar rolled to her feet and moved after her opponent.

Reaching his second possibility, Merlin turned onto his back, "Stop."

Sliding to a stop, Lazar looked at the Beretta in Merlin's hands. She grinned, slowly pulling the dress up her thighs as she rotated slightly on the balls of her feet, getting ready to strike, "Tuur already tried that. You have made your last mistake."

Shaking his head, Merlin said, "No. This is—"

Lazar must have recognized his confidence because her eyes flashed concern. She growled and lashed out with a kick.

Squeezing on the trigger, Merlin felt the pain in his fingers as her foot struck. A single gunshot exploded. The Beretta bounced across the cork floor.

Red blossoming on her left arm, Lazar's body jerked from the pain and her eyes shot open in surprise.

Merlin had one chance left. Ignoring his numb hand, he scissored his legs around hers and twisted hard.

Lazar's back hit the floor with a thud. There was the sound of air expelled from her lungs.

As she tried to roll away, Merlin snaked an arm around her neck, secured it with his other hand and squeezed. Hard. "Give it up."

She wouldn't. Lazar fought to tear his arm away. She lashed out with her bare legs. She threw elbows and tried to get at his face with her fingernails. Fight, fight, fight.

It took nearly a full minute before the fighting lessened. And then stopped. Merlin held his arm firmly around her neck, waiting for movement. Nothing. He released his arm slightly and checked her neck for a pulse. Dead. Struggling to his feet, sore from head to toe, Merlin retrieved the weapon and slipped it into his conceal holster. Then he moved across the room to check on Peeters.

Peeters jerked and his eyes opened in fear when he felt hands on his legs. When he saw it was Merlin, he looked around the room and spotted Lazar. His voice was filled with pain, "Is she...?"

"Yeah. Where's your bathroom?"

Gesturing weakly off to the left, Peeters said, "Just...just down the hall."

Merlin retrieved a towel from the bathroom and wrapped it around Peeters' lower leg.

Peeters glanced over at the body again, then looked at Merlin, "What...what are you going to do with me? We had a deal, right?"

Staying silent, Merlin stemmed the flow of blood.

"I know what you think of me, but–"

"I don't want to hear it. Just make sure you do that call on Constable Powless. And make sure that Colonel Leneave understands there was only one assassin. And it's not me. Get it?"

"Yes, yes, of course."

Merlin stood up, "I'll call an ambulance for you on my way out–"

"No. It is better if I call my aide," Peeters said. "My cell phone is in the bedroom. If you can...?"

Merlin moved quickly, still not trusting the man. He returned and dropped the cell phone to the politician's lap, "Yeah, I'm sure you'll want to cover this up."

Nodding, Peeter said, "For once we agree on something."

Striding to the door, Merlin put his hand on the doorknob. Another important matter came to him. He turned and looked at Peeters, "I want you to keep in mind I still have the recording."

Peeters nodded his head wearily, waving for Merlin to leave.

"Good. And since we have an understanding, I need you to do one more thing for me."

Chapter 55

PARIS, FRANCE

MERLIN'S ENTIRE BODY felt like one big ache. But he wasn't going to miss this for anything in the world. The cabaret was packed, busy and noisy, but sitting at his front row table, even in a disguise of heavy black beard, bushy eyebrows, and green contact lenses, Merlin felt like he was under a spotlight. Peeters had reached out to the French government, using some of his political capital to convince them he was working on behalf of another government in Interpol who needed their help. The French Minister of Justice worked directly with Sonny MacRae - Merlin used the character's name from one of last year's blockbuster novels - and Merlin convinced Monsieur Alexandre to let him put two agents undercover in a minor sting to ferret out a government employee spending government money on wine, women, and song. It was a dumb plan - one Alexandre really didn't buy but he went along with it - but it was also risky, maybe exposing his role as The Stopper in a needless way. But Merlin was determined to repay Captain Charity Sherrell and Captain Faith Saab for trusting him and putting everything on the line. Actually, he had thought he was calling their bluff. That they were only kidding. Turns out, they were not.

Trying to relax, Merlin took in the amazing decor of the Moulin Rouge The original place had burned down over one hundred years ago but this cabaret still held a colorful, rich history. The scent of French cuisine and wine was intoxicating. Music started and a French announcer came over the public address system. A moment later, there were screams, yelp and whoops as the famous Can-Can dance started.

The line of women came running front and center, already lifting and vigorously manipulating their red, white, and blue dresses and flashing their white underwear and contrasting black stockings.

Sherrell and Saab were the last two onto the dance floor.

Merlin's face nearly broke with the smile he couldn't contain. These two Canadian Air Force pilots, who had put life and limb on the line for him in the past, were having the time of their life. This was their way of dealing with the pressure of the job, letting off steam. Their Can-Can dancing wasn't quite as professional as the others but the delight they showed in the kicks, spins, and splits was very evident. But the ability for Sherrell and Saab to hold one leg high and grasping it by the ankle as they rotated just like the others was impressive. The biggest laugh - including from Merlin himself - came when the women lined up, bent over and threw their skirts over their backs, presenting their bottoms to the audience. Both Sherrell and Saab had a heart embroidered on the seat of her drawers and they wiggled their bottoms with abandon.

On the flight home, both Sherrell and Saab returned to the role of professional soldiers. But not without teasing him, claiming they knew he was watching them closer than the others and had turned red on a number of occasions. He refused to answer but felt his face burning as they headed for the cockpit.

A call from Constable Samantha Powless when they were over the ocean helped him to relax. And when she told him she had already talked to Director Laurent and O'Toole, and that they were going to recover completely, he was able to finally fall asleep.

Chapter 56

OTTAWA, CANADA

IT WAS JUST AFTER SUNUP when Merlin arrived home, struggling to carry his go-bag and a large shopping bag. He was dead tired - but not dead-dead, which was important- but his muscles pleaded for gallons of liniment and a deep massage with every step.

Jaimie's apartment door opened and his blue, woolly Chartreux cat scrambled down the hall. Ignoring his body's warnings, Merlin dropped his go-bag and the shopping bag, squatted and opened his arms, "Hey, pal? Did you miss me? I missed you." His muscles protested even under the weight of the cat as Jigs leaped into his arms but Merlin didn't care. He wrapped his arms around his best buddy.

Jigs cuddled and began purring.

Jaime was already halfway to him, running a hand through her jet black hair as Jigs flashed one of his brilliant Chartreux smiles at her, "That cat doesn't pine for you but I can definitely tell he misses you."

Merlin took in her orange jumpsuit and marveled at how she looked good in anything. And he had missed her as well. Something he knew he should say. "Thanks again for taking care of Jiggsy. And I–"

Jamie's bright blue eyes lit up and she bent over the shopping bag, "Hey? Did you bring me a gift?"

"Uh, yeah."

"I thought that looked like a dress."

Merlin had brought her something but he suddenly decided it wasn't a good idea. "But...it's not...the right...thing...and I'll bring it to you when I get the right...thing...."

Jamie lifted the red, white, and blue dress from the bag, "Okay, but for now I appreciate the thought." She looked over the material, "It's a little gaudy but....."

"Uh, yeah. Well, like I say–"

"Excuse me?" Jaime reached down and lifted a pair of frilly white bloomers from the bag. Her blue eyes blinked.

Merlin reached up for them with one hand as he cuddled Jigs.

But Jaime kept him from getting them, dropped them back in the bag, and pulled out a pair of dark nylon stockings. She blinked again and gestured with them to Merlin, "Seriously?"

"Uh...well...I happened to be in France and...well...it's a Can-Can outfit...and I know how you like to dance and–"

Jaime raised an eyebrow, "Couples dancing, mister. Couples dancing." She held the stockings out to him, a stern look on her face, "This is some man's fantasy. This is some man wanting to see my legs in sexy nylon stockings *and* getting me to lift my skirt so he can see my knickers at the same time."

"Uh...sorry–"

A big grin broke across Jaime's face, "And it's about time, Merlin Dragon. I was wondering if you had any fantasies about me." She knelt down and stuffed everything back in the bag before leaning and kissing his lips warmly. She looked into his eyes, "There will be only *one* person who ever sees my performance in this outfit."

"Your mother?"

Jaime tapped his nose with a finger, "Very funny. But you're not talking me out of it. I *will* fulfill your fantasy about me."

"I wasn't—"

"Uh-uh. I know you, Mr. Dragon. You will second guess everything in case you make a faux pas socially." She stood up, "You bring the wine and I'll bring the entertainment." She winked at him, turned, and jogged excitedly back down the hallway. She looked back when she reached her open door and called out, "Oh, but it can't do it for two weeks. I have to go to New York to see a client. But then...." She gave him a heel kick and disappeared inside her apartment.

Merlin massaged Jigs on the head with his fingers as he contemplated the closed door, "I *think* that went well, pal. My only problem is - what will she expect from me when she does dance the Can-Can? How am I supposed to act?"

Jigs chirped, jumped down from Merlin's arms and headed for their own apartment door.

Oh, that's just great, buddy. You're the only man-about-town that I know and you're going to leave me on my own without any kind of advice?

Don't miss out!

Visit the website below and you can sign up to receive emails whenever Eugene Lloyd MacRae publishes a new book. There's no charge and no obligation.

https://books2read.com/r/B-A-AC-QLFW

BOOKS 2 READ

Connecting independent readers to independent writers.

Did you love *Assassin*? Then you should read *Box Set: Rory Mack Steele Thrillers Books 1-12* by Eugene Lloyd MacRae!

Now in a single box set - 855,000 words - the first twelve action-packed thrillers in the Rory Mack Steele series. Like fast-paced thrillers? Then you'll love to go along with Private Detective Rory Mack Steele and his sister Skye Steele in a set of adventures that will keep you turning the pages.

Read more at eugenelloydmacrae.com.

Also by Eugene Lloyd MacRae

A Rory Mack Steele Novel
Betrayal
Storm
Hunted
Fire Plague
The Echelon Mind
The Chinese President
Knights of The Golden Circle
Cruise
Mask
The Overstolz Code
City
Stealing a Country
Jewel
Box Set: Rory Mack Steele Thrillers Books 1-12

Bulldog Malone
The Diamond Heist
The Banker Case
The Missing Case

The Stopper Files
Iron Pipeline
Economic Hitman
The Gunrunner
Assassin
Dark Money

Whiskey Empire
King of the Bootleggers
Gangsters
'Ndrangheta
Vendetta
Burn Powder
King of the Bootleggers Box Set

Watch for more at eugenelloydmacrae.com.